Praise for Sunset Street

This is a deep and meaningful story about family, getting second chances, and finding your way out of tragedy. Alero Smith makes one mistake that lands her in traumatic events in her life. If sympathy were dollars, Allie would have all of mine. It was unbelievable what the character was forced to go through, and the journey along with her was poignant and meaningful. She was a very flawed character, and the majority of the book was spent watching her grow, and figure out how to get her stuff together.

~ Susan K., Ontario, California

Sunset Street is a powerful story of a woman who overcame all odds. Alero was a Clinical Psychologist and an attorney who specialized in family and divorce. It is her story of how abuse spilled over into her daily life, of the legal battle she endured, and of the lessons that she learned so harshly from it all. It is her story; a story that will blast apart any preconceived notions you may have before you open this book. Sunset Street is a story about redemption and about change. The characters are compelling and it's a wonderfully meaningful piece that will appeal to anyone with the semblance of a heart.

~ Marwan Smith, Los Angeles

Sunset Street also is a work of fiction story covering important socio-political and cultural issues, and was penned by the author. More important than ever in light of the events of this past year, this story piece takes us through some of the key factors of color and race movement, both now and in its earlier stages. I feel like it was also written in tribute to those who have raised their voices and acted for those whose lives have been taken away, the work puts forth its narrative of questioning power, holding those in authority accountable, and standing up against oppression even if it's not your personal experience.

~ Kayode K., Lagos

Sunset Street was really being one of the most powerful books I have ever read; it is relatable and it is harsh but it is real life and that never runs smoothly. Akindotun Merino has written a very open, honest and deeply revealing story. This book shows that nothing is ever as cut and dried as it may seem from the start, that sometimes there just may be a deeper reason why something has happened. This is a story that is written from the heart. It was easy to read in terms of flow and the way it was written, just a difficult subject to get to grips with. The author has clearly taken a great deal of time and much effort to write this story.

~ Pamela S., United Kingdom

Sunset Street is a moving, honest and intimate book that reaches out to readers and is helpful to many out there who have experienced suffering and trauma in life. The book takes readers on a spiritual journey of healing and many will find inspiration in it. Every individual's journey is unique and different and this story also provides healing support to everyone. The authors' approach and honesty while dealing with difficult situations by the character is commendable and they reiterate God's nearness and presence in everyone's life.

~Aderonke K., Los Angeles, Ca

Trauma can have lasting effects in one's life, making one feel helpless and not knowing where to turn for help. The book gives a positive message on how God hears all our cries. The book is useful to all those who are undergoing problems in life as it helps them relate and inspired. The solutions in the story given are helpful to all. This story reaches out to readers who are suffering from trauma, emotional or physical abuse. It's an inspiration story for everyone who has lost hope and it helps them reconnect with God. The book is handy for all those women who are traumatized and hurt, and looking to recover.

~ Rebecca Adediran, Attorney/Writer

The plotline has a good twist which is unique. From living the life of a young and cherished child who had the world at her feet, Alley moves on to see the darker sides of live and must scale through without losing herself. Marriage becomes an issue she has to tumble through, but she comes out stronger and better and eventually marries a childhood friend. There was every touch of suspense as there was also a resolution of the climax built. I consider this work a great read. I rate it a 4 out of 4 stars and the author's narrative technique appealed to me. I highly recommend this novel to all lovers of historical and romance fiction.

~ David Longhouse, Houston, Texas

This is a very moving story, an experience that one can never seem to forget in a lifetime. This book "Sunset Street" is very interesting and will help the reader to shape his/her life in other to know how to go along with life. I am among the lucky ones to have read this story, though, my experience tends to be different.

~ Kylie, O., Artist

Excellent story and wonderful writing! You were able to develop such a nostalgic feeling for your readers with your writing. At times it really became a coming-of-age story. This family was endearing and it was so interesting to see their story play out. You also intertwined historical events into the story nicely. I don't know for sure but I would not be surprised if you based this novel on your own family or people that you know.

~ Mrs. Poulson, New Jersey

Also by: Akindotun Merino

Academic Success
Souls Desire
Bathtub Therapy
The Perfect Gift of a Mother
The Perfect Fit Approach to Finding Your Mate
The Keys to Forgiveness & Miracles: Secrets of the Sages.

SUNSET STREET

AKINDOTUN MERINO

BLUEPRINT PRESS
INTERNATIONALE

Sunset Street

Copyright © 2022 by Akindotun Merino

ISBN
978-1-959365-43-3 (Paperback)
978-1-959365-44-0 (eBook)
978-1-959365-42-6 (Hardcover)

To the one who makes my heart sing and to all those fortunate to find their song.

To Mother Ilean - for your love and care! I'll miss you till forever.

Ife (love)

You are my past that lives today
Ever present in the unfolding
Life's compass and measuring tool
My day and night
Song on replay
I remember Ife (love)
Laughter shattered the silence
Holding hands under the Mango tree
Making love on the Serengeti,
You crawled into my soul and made a home.
Kisses flutter
Hands tracing bodies
You reach deeper
I exhale!
Ife!

~ Akindotun

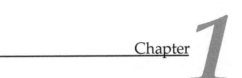

Chapter 1

My name is Alero Smith. People call me Allie or Allie Pooh. Only Pop calls me the latter. Momma is not the type to go around calling people elaborate pet names; for her, the simplest approach will do just fine. It's a name that belonged to princesses from the Itsekiri ethnic group in Nigeria. I'm Allie Pooh to Pop and then later to the one man who fills my bones with love. I happened to like school and couldn't get enough information to answer all the questions on my mind. The teachers didn't like me asking too many questions but how were you supposed to learn without inquiry? My homework was never late, my work was stellar, and I even found time to bring the teacher an apple.

I was a loved child, the product of Pop and Momma's young love. It was the kind that found its way through the thicket and brambles of mangled forest. It was the type of love that crept through thickets and brambles until it found two lights in the Deep South. The type of love that sings in Grand Central station without ticket fare. It found its way to Pop and Momma, a couple of Black folks who couldn't have purchased this love with all the funds in the Treasury. The kind of love that settles inequities, that cannot be marginalized or purchased. Pop and Momma spread their wings and took flight together. I crawled out of their happy space, sheltered from the brutal heat of life.

Tolah, Momma—tall and lithe like a gazelle, a caramel-toned woman exuding the splendor of queens. Momma Smith, as she was fondly addressed in the neighborhood even by those old enough to be her mother, made sure her love overflowed to the community. I loved when she threw her head back and belched out that full-throttle laughter, the kind with enough power to pierce the darkest space. The light of Momma Smith kept folks alive. The story was told of the little girl who lived next to us. She was playing catch with her brother when she tripped, and hit her head on the concrete floor. She was unconscious and everyone stood in shock as they waited for an ambulance. It was at that moment that Momma and her friend were walking back from the store and something funny must have been said because Momma busted out laughing; her laughter carried and floated to Danielle's unconscious body. Danielle opened her eyes. It could be a coincidence, but the entire neighborhood ascribed the little girl's consciousness to Momma's laughter. Danielle said she heard Momma's laughter from a distance and wanted to laugh with her.

Momma was also the beloved math teacher who made home visits to teach math lessons. Momma was the type to offer suggestions on fruit selection to her students in the grocery store or help a boy with his tie on the way into church. She was tough but would get that math in her students' head and get them doing stuff without a calculator or pen and paper. She was the best math teacher on this side of town. Momma had a chest of drawers stuffed with awards to honor her hard work. I often wondered why she never displayed them for people to see what an accomplished woman she was. Her students loved her. Her community sung her praises, but Momma was more interested in instilling a good education to her students and had no time for grandiosities. Momma breathed life into others and her lungs expanded even wider to resuscitate those close to her.

James Smith, my father—tall, dark, and handsome, with enough swagger to light any room. Pop was my first love. I was his princess, who could do no wrong. He was the builder extraordinaire who owned his own construction company, Smith Construction, and took pride in working hard to provide for his family. Pop feared God and conducted everything in accordance with his directives, or should I say the directives Pop deemed fitting. But I liked his God. He seemed to modify himself according to the situation, so if Pop slipped in his quest to stop smoking, his God met him with Grace. Pop's God didn't usually agree with all the pastor preached on Sundays. When the pastor admonished all the women to wear hats to church or not hold a post in the church because they were the lesser human, Pop didn't think that had anything to do with God but was just a misguided human interpretation of him. He went faithfully to church but didn't concern himself with telling the pastor when he agreed or didn't. Pop's God allowed someone like me, a little girl, to hope and dream to become anything I dared to become. Pop wore his faith with pride, a man of honor and integrity. He breathed his family, especially his Momma, the royal queen of his castle. He was sure to open doors for her. I remember a time when he was removing stuff from the car and Mom opened the door herself to save time. Pop, in that gentle "Tolah" voice, reproached, "Baby, you should have waited, you are so worth the wait."

From that moment, Momma slowed her hurried frequency to match her husband's pace. He took care of her as if worshipping her and you could be certain that Pop's God gave allowance for this. He told me that all the accolades we ascribed to this heavenly being were made flesh in his wife. She was his love, joy, patience, and adoration. Pop played the guitar, one that he'd picked up from a bet. He wasn't a gambling man, but he would bet on a game and if someone was foolish enough to bet a guitar, well, Pop took it and gave thanks the next Sunday. Pop played his guitar and sung the newest verse he'd written for Tolah, complete with her sitting on his lap, which you'd think would have made for an uncomfortable venture, but it didn't stop him. Momma sat across him while he extended the guitar and his arms to sing the next new song.

He took his family to church every Sunday and led prayer every morning and night at our home. He also read literature on other world religions. He believed there could be consensus in the human search for a deity. He built houses across Southern California. Pop was charismatic, with a deep Luther Vandross–type voice that charmed, the life of any party. According to Tolah, he had friends from here to Timbuktu. When Pop entered a room, the world wanted to stand at attention. Black folks loved this, but it made the white folks fear him. But Pop tried to disarm them at all times. Whenever a white policeman pulled him over for what always was a false reason, Pop was ready. He knew there was no reason to pull him over since he drove at the speed limit, was sure his insurance and license were updated. Momma and Pop prided themselves on leaving nothing to chance, or I should say that Momma left nothing to chance. Pop would drive without a license left to his own devices, but Momma wouldn't permit it. When he got pulled over, he confidently said, "Hello, Officer, how is your day going?" By the time Pop was finished, the officer had been invited to our Saturday picnic. Not that any of them showed up, but Pop could disarm anyone despite themselves. Pop had his own faults, but I didn't see them. I'm sure Momma would paint a different picture, one not so clean of her James, but I'm writing this story, so you should believe me.

Pop and Momma were originally from Grenada, Mississippi, a segregated township that shaped them.They grew up in the same neighborhood during the struggle for black survival. Grandpa Smith was an itinerant preacher who moved from city to city to preach and got enough to send money to his wife and five children. Pop, being the oldest, became the man of the house by the age of ten. His best friend, to the embarrassment of his friends, was my mother, his Tolah, who lived down the street. They would hide and eavesdrop on adult conversations, which was how they overhead Grandma Mabel tell her girlfriend that her husband might be using preaching as a ruse and had been drafted as a civil rights officer.

"Are you sure?"

"How could I be sure?" Grandma Mabel responded. "But I looked through some of the papers on the table the last time he was here, and it was frightening."

"Oh Jesus."

"That man will get us killed."

The two frightened ladies held hands and they shivered at the thought of Grandpa Smith getting lynched for his involvement. Pop and Momma did the same, as the thought of Grandpa hanging by a rope like those they saw at least once a week on the way to the school was enough to make any child want to throw up. I once overheard Pop share a story of a young man whom he'd watched die on a tree. The boy's throat had been slit open in several places. Like someone had been trying to sever his head only to remember he needed it for the hanging. He'd seen two types of blood— one was bright red and the other a deep red—both racing to run down the man's half-naked body, down his legs, to be swallowed by the Mississippi soil. A soil that was red from the stains of thousands of unrighteous bloodsheds in the state. In my Sunday school class, we read a story about the blood of Abel crying out to God because he'd been killed unjustly. I sometimes wondered why the blood of Black folks who were killed did not cry out for vengeance. And if it did, why did the earth not respond?

One day after school, Pop heard a wail coming from the house, the type that shatters innocence. Before he got consumed by that wail, he ran towards Momma's house, where she was skipping rope. She looked up, dropped her rope, and ran to meet him. Pop grabbed his friend's right hand with his left and they both ran back towards his house. By this time, the entire neighborhood had packed into the tiny house. The two found their way to Grandma Mabel, who was still rolling on the floor, screaming inconsolably.

Pop said, "That day, I held on to your mother's hand and saw the tears falling like rain. She did the crying for me."

"Pop, you didn't cry when your father died?"

"Not right then he didn't," Momma chimed in.

Pop continued with the story, "I gathered my brothers and sisters and started making dinner. That was until Aunty Vivian came into the kitchen and shooed me out of the way like I didn't know what I was doing. I figured life must go on and Mom was doing all the mourning for all of us. That day, I officially became the man of the house."

Fast forward a few years later to our escape to California. "Your father's grief gave way to tears on our drive from Jackson to California. He pulled off the road and started howling. I was afraid something had happened to him.

"'Are you sick, James? Are you all right? What happened?' I asked. But he simply kept on crying. It then occurred to me that he was weeping for his father.

"I asked again, 'James, is this about your pa?' And he nodded yes. I got out of the car and climbed on the trunk, waiting for his sobs to subside."

"Momma, why did you have to leave the car?"

"A man is entitled to grieve in private."

I could picture all of it in my mind's eye, Momma sitting on the back of the car with her feet hanging down. Hoping no police would drive by to disturb her new husband's grief.

When I was in high school, I wrote to some of Pa's contacts and a man by the name of Joe responded. I was eighteen years old with a loud voice and needed an outlet away from Mississippi. I was told by our pastor that every man was needed in this cause. I was ready. We all heard Fannie Lou Hamer say, 'If I fall, I'll fall five feet four inches forward in the fight for freedom.' I was ready to give my life for freedom. The struggle continues."

"Pop was liable to get himself killed and I was not going to allow that."

"How could you have stopped him?"

"Well, I packed my bags and followed him."

"Yeah, your mother was as stubborn as a mule. She still is," he teased. "She looked at me and whispered in that you-better-not-mess-with-me-today voice, 'James Bartholomew Smith, if you think I'll let you leave Mississippi without me, you better have another thought. You ain't leaving me here by myself. I'm coming with you.'"

"You are in trouble when she says your entire name, Pop."

"You got that right, Allie Pooh."

"But that was it," Momma continued. "we became the best recognizance team on this side of the Mississippi."

"It turned out Momma was just as radical as me. She didn't understand why we had to sit in the back of buses or drink from separate water fountains when the same water came out of both. "Your mother was the starter and closer. People were more receptive to what I had to say once Momma had made them comfortable. I always introduced her as my sister, and we had fun with that."

Momma laughed. "Remember the time we left that house and the man said, 'Take care of your sister, you hear?'" She turned to me, "He decided to come out of his house as your father was kissing me. We saw him and ran while he rained curses on your father."

They both started laughing. The kind of laughter where you throw your head back and let it ring. It was so contagious that I joined mine with theirs.

I was sharing a bit of their Mississippi journey. Like a caterpillar shedding its skin, my parents had escaped their captivity. Their laughter was a diaphragm that sucked up their burdens and those of their parents before them, all the way back through the Jim Crow South, enveloping all the hate. Momma and Pop were left standing together.

Chapter 2

We were the first in our neigborhood to purchase a home. And even before that, life was good. Pop, Momma, and I basked in a cocoon that protected me from the dangers in our neighborhood. It wasn't uncommon to wake up to dead bodies saturated with drive-by bullets in the neighborhood. Other times some dropped dead on the sidewalk from drug overdoses. To tell the truth, I had more protection than Pop and Momma. It was Mother Harris who walked the streets yelling for the drug dealers to leave her children alone, myself included. All the children in the neighborhood belonged to Mother Harris. She was the matriarch, stout and frumpy with piercing eyes that seemed to see in all directions. Mother Harris knew when a drive-by was about to happen. She prayed loudly in her apartment and once you heard, "Oh thank you, Jesus," you could expect a revelation of what was happening in Little Africa, as our apartment building was affectionately known. She would warn mothers to keep their children in the house because some men possessed by Satan himself would smear the ground with blood this evening. All learned to listen to Mother Harris because her foretelling always seemed like déjà vu. She was almost always right. When she predicted that that there would be an exodus of white people, we expected all the whites to all of a sudden get on a bus that would transport them out of Little Africa. That didn't happen. Instead, the white exodus from the neigbhorhood was gradual. It happened in drips, almost as if nothing was happening. It was noticing that Ms. Lilly no longer attended church or that the Andrew children hadn't been on the bus yesterday. Until one day, we realized that almost all were gone and that Mother Harris had been right. She was afforded the respect due to a mother of her stature, even from the hard-core drug dealers. Mother Harris's home was a safe place for me. Her one-bedroom apartment was located across the tiny basketball court. Mother Harris could see all that happened in Little Africa. There were no children or grandchildren around Mother Harris and I asked her once about her lack of progeny. She simply said, "They are all dead!" No explanation as she kept knitting her scarf, needles pulling yellow, green, and teal yarn into formation. I sat on the carpet, watching and waiting for one of her life lessons but today the only word that floated in the air was *death*. After a while, she said, "Death is a family member that comes visiting each of us. She's nothing to be feared. You see, she seemly comes to guide us home."

"Why is death a she?" I asked.

"I'd rather remember her as a mother helping her child. It's more comforting that way," she explained. "So there is a need to live intentionally, fully, and gracefully. Embrace all because one day death will appear. Mother Death!"

I didn't know what to say. Here I was, sitting on a frayed brown carpet listening to Mother Harris explain that my life was on loan. I didn't want to live a life that was loaned to me. I wanted to own my life. How could I go about owning myself without the imminent coming of Mother Death? Maybe I could bargain with her. Not that I didn't ever want to die but I didn't want death to appear before I'd enjoyed all the good things like graduation, a wedding, driving my own car, travel, and so much more. It didn't seem fair that death could simply show up without warning or notice. It seemed to me that we should all have signed contracts with loan terms like I heard Momma and Pop talk about. Death would stipulate how long the lease was for and, if I agreed, then we'd sign but if I didn't, there would be room for negotiation.

Death could say something like, "Allie, your life is on loan for fifty-nine years."

Then I would say, "That is not acceptable, because by fifty-nine my children will have just started having children and I don't want my grandchildren to be without a grandmother. You know they are vital to the development of children."

I'd expect Death to see the reason in this and say something like, "That seems reasonable, we can add twenty more years to make it seventy-nine."

"But seventy-nine is an odd number, Death," I would continue. "Why not make it eighty-six?"

"Why eighty-six?" Death would ask.

"Because eighty-six says Death was fair. That you allowed me to grow old, long enough to live a legacy but not too long to be a burden. I like eighty-six."

"Deal!"

Pop lived transactionally and I wouldn't be surprised if he'd already made his life bargain. He made time to talk to the dealers and explain the price that was paid for them to express such choices. We came to know the dealers by name, Big for Sho, Harris the Blow, and Catch the Bus were some of the standout nicknames. They would yell out to me as I was always sandwiched between Pop and Momma, "Hey, shorty, how was school?" "Stay in your studies," "Don't do drugs." They addressed my parents respectfully, "Hello, Mr. and Mrs. Smith," "Have a nice day." Pop would address each by name, their real names, "Good afternoon, Mr. Johnson! Good afternoon, Mr. Williams!" He would say good afternoon until each person had been recognized. These neighborhood gang members would high-five each other as my father repeated their names like they were being called to receive awards.

The exodus called white flight was followed by Black professionals leaving the community. Pop said that white people had been raptured or abducted from the neighborhood since we hadn't seen them leave. Even Mrs. Popon, the nice lady across the street, left without saying goodbye. We woke up one day to a community void of whiteness. Even Scott, the homeless veteran, had fled. Pop said they'd probably dragged him kicking and screaming since Scott loved him some homemade fried chicken that folks here offered him freely. Pop prayed and worked towards his own exodus like the white folks. We continued to live in Little Africa until Pop and Momma saved enough money to get us out.

We packed all our belongings into the orange-and-white U-Haul truck, which Pop had rented for two days. Momma and Pop were proud to have that U-Haul spend the night in front of our apartment, a symbol of their transition to a better life. We woke up to see it surrounded by Big for Sho and his group. There were about ten Black men stationed around the U-Haul. Momma asked if Pop had asked them to do this but the surprised look on his face answered the question. When the gang saw us coming towards them, they took two rehearsed steps forward and raised their caps in salutation. I was speechless. In the excitement of moving, my parents had forgotten that U-Hauls were stolen around here. This group of drug dealers and gangbangers had shown their appreciation for Pop Smith by guarding his U-Haul. I learned a lesson that day, that light can penetrate the darkest night, and that night in San Bernardino, that light shined brightly.

The move was a status change for my parents. We were one of the few that made it out of Little Africa. My parents had saved enough money for a down payment in what folks around there called a professional community. We were moving to Sunset Street, where there was no grafitti on the walls. Our new neighborhood had palm-lined streets and a neighborhood watch, and the people who lived there people were business owners or doctors, teachers, engineers, literary agents, and so on. A move up by one was celebrated by all, and the entire neighborhood came to bid us goodbye. We were their promise, a down payment of sorts that if the Smiths could make it out, they would too.

The late 1970s were troubling times for Black folks, Latinos, and some immigrants. Pop said the Watergate scandal would be the end of Nixon's presidency and it was. It wasn't so much what he did with those tapes, it was the lying that torpedoed him. "God don't like ugly" was Pop's declarative sentence. It's funny how Pop always weaved God into his thoughts, yet church folks would say he was a hooligan. To add to that were all these Black men dying in Vietnam and coming home in body bags. How were we equal enough to die, yet the Black underclass continued to define all Black men in America? This was one of those rhetorical questions Momma said needed no response since the answers were glaringly obvious; we asked them just to make a point. I don't quite like rhetorical questions because they keep people guessing. We might think we know the answer, or we could have different ones. As for creating a dramatic effect, I can think of better ways than tying such flare to questions. A question should be answered, period, not used as a punch line. I am of the mind that clear and distinct communication leaves no room for assumptions. But what did I know at that age? It's easier said from the purview of adulthood.

People were dissatisfied with their government and each other. There was distrust of the American dream. Inflation was at an all-time high by the end of Jimmy Carter's presidency. I heard Momma and Pop talking about good men who sometimes couldn't handle the presidency. Meaning that President Carter was too good to succeed. My young mind couldn't understand the dichotomy in my parents asking me to be a good girl if it would only lead to failure.

The Black community faced tremendous pressure during this time. Poverty is much more than a lack of money or work or even motivation. For many marginalized groups, it is the result of a generational history of struggles, lack of opportunities and access, institutional racism, and lack of mentorship. There was an influx of Blacks and Mexicans who moved from Los Angeles to the suburbs of San Bernardino and Riverside Counties. Homes were affordable and renting there was still cheaper than LA. We were one of the families to settle in San Bernardino County in search of a better life.

Life before the move was not horrible because of the love Pop and Momma built around me. Like a warm fireplace, my life was warmed from the cold world outside our walls. The subsidized housing of Little Africa ensured that we were housed with some who had multiple jobs and others who refused to work because they were strung out on drugs. There were drug dealers and prostitutes, but they all looked up to my parents, whose passion for hard work and education resulted in a Saturday school taught by Momma and an entrepreneurial workshop taught by Pop. At first, people were skeptical, but the Smiths kept showing up on Saturdays and would go door to door asking parents to come down for just an hour to learn about what their children were learning in schools and for their children to bring homework or any subject they struggled with to the Saturday Academy, as it would later be called. Soon there were twenty or more regulars and sometimes they would have eighty students in the multipurpose room. Momma invited other teachers from the neighborhood to assist. News spread quickly and the district heard about Momma and Pop's success with this group and offered to help.

Each Saturday, the school district brought food and school supplies. The police department joined in the venture and paraded the area so we could have school undisturbed. Pop's entrepreneurial workshops were just as successful. He taught students how to set up their own business and build savings for their families. He helped men open bank accounts and made them accountable to each other. My parents won several awards from the city and county of San Bernardino. I was right there with them, learning and organizing and teaching children younger than myself how to read. However, we were aware how dangerous the streets were getting and my parents wanted me to grow up in a safer environment. Pop promised to provide for me what he'd always wanted—clean streets, a nice house with a picket fence, and neighbors who didn't sell drugs.

My parents and I would crowd around the small dining table at the end of each month and watch Pop calculate the total savings. If it had increased from the last month, we would dance and whoop and walk to Mr. Lee's store for some Nestlé ice cream sandwiches. We walked back holding hands and sometimes I walked behind to watch my parents walk together, Pop's hand resting on the small of Momma's back. They acted like teenagers and their love drew me in. I wore their love like a warm winter robe. They planted a seed that sprouted and took root.

I would miss my friends Ebony, or Eb, and Shade, whom we called Shades. We were the three divas and planned to take on the world. We read encyclopedias, competed on the spelling team, and biked to the Chinese store down the block on Fridays. Eb would become a Hollywood actress; I would become a therapist and civil rights attorney fighting for the marginalized; Shades would become a business tycoon, making all the money her family never had. Eb had one of those faces that you can't forget, with her almond eyes and thick black hair. She was certainly the most beautiful girl on our street and at the school and the way the boys flocked around her got her mom nervous. She was forever yelling warnings like, "Eb don't need to be walked home. Go home to your parents!" Eb would walk right by her mom with a sheepish smile and say something like, "Don't mind them, Ma. I didn't ask to be walked. I'm not a dog!" Indeed, Eb never asked but she reveled in the attention like a fish in the water. Eb lived with her mom and stepdad and brother. They had a relatively happy life and her stepdad was good to her. Eb's parents were also saving to get out of Little Africa. They seemed to have a bit more money than us because Eb always had expensive new gadgets and clothes. She was spoiled but not a brat. It was the kind of "the world revolves around me but I want you in my world so it can revolve around all of us" spoiled. She was a giver and believed in the goodness in her world. Eb was unaware of the dangers in our neighborhood, including the drugs and drive-by shootings. Her head was forever stuck in a storyline, a book, movie, or television show. She was the Black Anne from *Anne of Green Gables* and would make us watch her perform. We teased her that Black folks didn't watch *Anne of Green Gables*, to which she shrugged and recited two of her favorite lines—"When I left Queen's, my future seemed to stretch out before me like a straight road. I thought I could see along with it for many a milestone. Now there is a bend in it. I don't know what lies around the bend, but I'm going to believe that the best does," and, "Why must people kneel down to pray? If I really wanted to pray I'll tell you what I'd do. I'd go out into a great big field all alone or in the deep, deep, deep woods, and I'd look up into the sky—up—up—up—into that lovely blue sky that looks as if there was no end to its blueness. And then I'd just *feel* a prayer."

She took a bow and we clapped because she was good. If you closed your eyes you would believe she was Anne. Eb would bring our reading stories to life in the classroom. When we sat in reading circles, Eb made sure she got up to read and when the teacher asked her to sit down, she would say, "But the character so much wants to be heard and she can't be with me sitting down." To which the entire classed laughed and Eb either kept acting out the reading or was made to sit, depending on the teacher. Some of our homeroom teachers, like Mr. Bathaway, encouraged Eb's proclivities and others, like Ms. Davies, almost crushed her spirit.

Shades was the light-skinned one among us, because her mom was Latina. However, her African father was not in the picture and she didn't know him. Eb always thought that was tragic not to have a father to imagine, so she'd created a dad for Shades. In our imagination, Shades' father was a Nigerian prince who'd had to return home to be king of his town because his father had died. He'd been given a wife and the new queen would not allow him to contact his beautiful American daughter. We would laugh at this story, which got more elaborate as we grew older, but it was all we had and I, for one, was glad that the story didn't make the man a prisoner or drug dealer. Shades had been named by her father and that was all her mother was willing to share. Shades was brilliant, the smartest of us three. She was always the top in the class, but more than that, Shades was so sweet and gentle. She would listen to Eb and I talk and never grow tired. She was like a sponge, soaking in the life of Little Africa. She was a ray of sunshine. Shades's smile could melt the hardest heart and she was so easy to love. Shades and I would walk holding hands or wrap our arms around each other for no other reason than that she was lovable. We would do this while Eb walked in front of us, walking backward so she could face us and tell stories or repeat jokes that made us howl laughing till the tears rolled down our faces. Money was always tight in Shades's house. There were four other siblings but none of the fathers stayed. They were in and out of the house like it was a hotel of sorts. I wondered why her mom kept getting pregnant, because her track record should have informed her decisions. Her mom worked three jobs and still couldn't make ends meet. Eb and I shared our clothes with Shades. We shared each other's clothes but we would 'forget' to get them back from Shades.

The three of us gathered each Friday and took turns spending the night in each other's home. When the girls were at my house we would stay in my room and the same at Eb's house, but we rarely spent the night at Shades's house because there were too many people and too little room. We looked forward to Fridays. I remember the time we went around stuffing our panties with toilet paper, waiting for the arrival of the bloody monthly period, a moment that would enshrine us in womanhood forever. We celebrated Eb's womanhood, when it came first, by eating some chicken offered to the gods on her behalf. Eb later shared the story of how a chicken had been sacrificed so she could live. It was a tale we all knew existed only in her mind but it fit our imaginary lives. Shades taught us how to French kiss. She said all we had to do was stick our tongue down each other's throats. She was our kissing coach. We took turns sticking our tongues down Shades's throat until we felt like puking. Shades said we would try again in a year, maybe we simply needed to grow into the kiss. We talked about our wedding day and who would be the maid of honor so—I would be Eb's and Shades would be mine and Ebony would be hers.

Most importantly we wanted to make a difference. I had caught the civil rights bug from my father, who'd caught it from his father before him, so I convinced the girls to form a social justice club in elementary school. We marched to Principal Dewitt's office and demanded to start a club as it was our right as students. He asked what type of club and I said, "A social justice club." Principal Dewitt handed us some papers and asked that we complete them and return them to his office. No further queries. No opportunity to rebut his opposition. This seemed too easy, until we read all the requests on the papers. First, we needed a purpose for the club and an instructor who would act as a sponsor and then a list of events and a budget. There were also the election of officers and descriptions of duties. These might all be daunting to other ten- and eleven-year-olds, but we decided to prove to Principal Dewitt that we would not be intimated by the eight pages of the application form. We found Miss Juanita Roberts, our homeroom teacher, who allowed us to stay in her class for lunch and discuss whatever topic we chose. We asked her and she said, "It would be my honor to sponsor this club." This was the most difficult step. After that, we huddled in Ms. Roberts's class during lunch for the next couple of days and on Wednesday, we submitted a typed application to Principal Dewitt. By the next month, we were approved to host our Social Justice Club. I was president, Eb was vice president, and Shades was secretary. We invited all our friends and they invited theirs and the first meeting of the SJ Club, as we were known, packed out Ms. Roberts's classroom, with standing room only. I rattled statistics for Blacks and minorities and how we needed to do all we could to change these horrible statistics by being the best students at the school. I don't remember much of what else was said but I remember the energy in the room and how parents started poking through the doors to listen. Eb spoke eloquently and was dressed like Angela Bassett, her Hollywood hero. Shades was quiet but took notes. Ms. Roberts beamed at the principal, who was speechless at the turnout. Someone must have taken pictures because the next week, our faces were plastered in the district newspaper. I felt proud that SJ Club took on issues like cafeteria food, toilet cleanliness, mean teachers, and so on. That club still exists on the campus today. The three of us made a pact to set our world ablaze with success. We pricked our index fingers with a safety pin and became blood sisters.

We vowed that my move wouldn't disrupt our friendship.

Our mothers promised not to interfere with our Friday gatherings, and it was a vow that held for the next two decades.

Chapter *3*

We moved to Sunset Street in the summer of 1992 on a bright, sunny San Bernardino day. It was as hot as the sun. Eb and Shades and I packed in the back of Momma's car while Pop drove the truck. We were racing to finish ice cream that was struggling to stay on the cone. It was a three-bedroom house that looked like those homes you see in the magazines. The street was lined with trees and there were children of different black and brown hues playing on the streets. We three girls looked at each other, baffled, until I asked Momma, "Why is no one watching these children?"

"They can see them from inside the house, plus this area is safe. They all watch out for each other. It's one of the reasons we selected this place."

"There is no graffiti, Mom," Shades noticed. We called each other's parents mom and dad. One of the decisions we made during one of our Friday discussions.

"Yeah, no graffiti," Momma whispered, as if she was awed by this news.

Our house was right by the hillside on something Momma referred to as the cul-de-sac, a word we looked up in our pocket dictionary. It's a French word that literally means the "bottom of the bag" and it refers to a street or passage closed at one end, a dead-end street, typically with a rounded end. Pop made good money and we could afford to live in a house by the hillside. We also noticed that the streetlights worked and that there were metal boxes in front of each of the homes. Momma said these were mailboxes for each home. A stand-alone mailbox, rather than a mail slot, signified that you had a piece of the American dream, so I ran to examine it. We noticed a red lever, which we kept raising up and down until Pop explained that the mail carrier knew to pick up outgoing mail when the red lever was raised. I fell in love with Sunset Street.

The entire Sunset neighborhood came out to welcome us. There were knocks on the door at intervals with someone bringing a cake or casserole, Jollof rice, or fried chicken and macaroni and cheese, not the kind from a box but the southern type with slightly browned cheese and crust on the top. The type you cut into and take a mouthful before getting a plate. The Martinezes brought tamales and Mrs. Lopez and her children brought some green chile enchiladas. Ebs, myself, and Shades simply stared at all the food and gifts as if Christmas were happening in July. We quickly found my room, which was a suite—I had my own bathroom attached to the room.

"This is bigger than your living room in the apartments," Eb yelled.

"Yes, I know," I responded as we walked the room.

"Let's have a picnic in here," Shades said.

"Great idea," we all exclaimed.

We walked into the kitchen and gathered as much food as we could carry and it looked like Momma didn't mind.

The moms and dads were unloading the truck, which needed to be returned to U-Haul that evening so Pop didn't have to pay for an extra day. It was common knowledge that Pop didn't believe in giving to big business unnecessarily. We could hear him tell Momma to attend to all the visitors because he had to unload this goddarn truck. It went something like this, "Go on and attend to these folks here. I must return this truck before 6:00 p.m."

"Okay, why don't you do that while the ladies and I arrange things around here!"

That's how my parents managed their lives, always a division of labor, partners in every way. I think they were happy that the children were out of the way. The girls and I went back to our room. After a while, Eb declared that we were wasting time in the room.

"Did you see all those cute boys on your street, Allie?"

"No, I didn't notice."

"Are you blind?" Shades asked. "There was the dark-chocolate one with the braided hair and the other mixed kid with curly hair."

"Thank you, sis," said Ebony, high-fiving Shades as if they had discovered the cure for cancer.

"Let's go outside!" They both declared so I had no choice but to be dragged outside. The boys immediately noticed us and walked our way.

"Hey welcome to Sunset," the dark-chocolate one said.

"Thank you," Eb responded as she moved towards him.

"I'm Ebony." She extended her hand, "And this is Shade and Allie."

"I'm Marshawn and my friend here is Calvin."

"So how is this place?" Eb asked.

"Good," they responded, feeling no need to explain.

"Do you play spades?" Marshawn asked.

"Yes," we replied.

"Allie will school you! You better not try it if you can't hang," Eb yelled.

"Well, Calvin here is a pro," responded Marshawn.

"Bring it on," Eb said, and we nodded. We were ready to take them on.

Marshawn and Calvin ran back to their home and came back with the cards.

"Do you both live in the same house?" Eb asked.

"Eb!" I cautioned, trying to signal for her to play it cool.

"It's okay. No, we don't," Calvin explained. "We live next door to each other, but we've been friends since we were three. Marshawn's home is like mine and mine his."

"Us too," Eb explained. "We've been friends since before we were born. Our parents are best friends and they were pregnant about the same time."

"Eb, too much information," I volunteered again.

It looked like this girl had lost her head to Marshawn and I saw that Calvin had already caught Shades's eye as they were having a different conversation away from us.

Just as I was about to say it might be time to go inside, Eb and Shades's moms came outside and told the girls it was time to leave. We completed our elaborate goodbye hug and I went into the house.

I found Momma and Pop laid out on each of the couches, so I threw myself on the floor and we all sighed in unison, then we start laughing, the kind of laugh that crawls out of your stomach happy until it spills into the atmosphere and draws a ring of joy around its inhabitants. Just then the doorbell rang, but we tried to ignore it. Its persistence forced laughter to recede to its corner. Momma and I went to receive our night visitor and in strolled a woman about my mother's age and her son, who looked to be about my age, holding a basket that overflowed with the kind of snacks Eb, Shades, and I salivated over in magazines and swore to eat every day when we grew up. I stared at Nordic potato chips, chestnut spread, stroopwafels from the Netherlands, and those Cadbury chocolate bars from the UK, and those were merely the snacks visible to me. This woman obviously didn't belong in this part of town. She seemed like one of those women who lounged in a Beverly Hills hotel sipping pomegranate martinis by the pool. The kind of woman who would eventually change into a power suit for a meeting with an executive. This lady, whoever she was, seemed to have stepped off the cover of *Ebony*. Her well-tailored dark mauve suit and open-toed six-inch stilettos replaced the forgone laughter with the sun. She was television gorgeous with rich caramel skin and long legs that belonged on a runway. For a moment we couldn't stop staring at this lady, whose smile lifted us closer to her world. We almost forgot her son was there until she pulled him forward.

"These are for you," she stated to no one as she proceeded to walk through the house like a seasoned visitor. Her son handed me the basket filled with all the expensive snacks.

I saw Momma and Pop from the corner of my eye giving each other strange looks. You know the type of look that's been developed over years of living within close walls. I knew they wanted to laugh but were too polite to do so. Ms. Washington would later become Momma's best friend but that evening, we all swallowed up our tiredness and she granted us a new source of energy for the night.

"Hello, I am Ms. Emelia Washington, your next-door neighbor. And here is my fabulous son, Adey. Pronounced like Abby but with a *d*." I thought that name fit her perfectly, Emelia, but we ended up calling her Ms. Washington.

Then she proceeded to walk to the room like a model.

"Hello, Ms. Washington. We are the Smiths. I am Tolah and this is my husband, James, and my daughter, Allie." Momma responded to save us from staring. There was a slight smile on Adey's face, as someone used to the effect of his mom's presence.

"Oh!" She pulled my mother into a tight hug like they were long-lost friends. "I am so glad to make your acquaintance. I have a feeling we will be very good friends."

She then hugged Pop and finally me.

"You are such a good-looking family." She assessed us like she was making a judgment then proceeded to say, "We will surely get along." Her final verdict. She wasn't condescending. She didn't make us feel small but reminded me of the kind of hospitality and brutal honesty my parents reminisced of back in Mississippi.

We smiled. Then Adey walked up to Pop with airs of authority too big for his age.

"Hello, Mr. Smith." He shook hands with Pop and did the same thing with myself and Momma.

The adults started talking. Ms. Washington had been a backup singer for Diana Ross and now had her own band, the Butterflies, which toured in Europe. This would explain the foreign snacks, I thought.

"You all have to come once you are settled. We are doing Luxembourg and Germany next month."

I was in awe as I watched this well-traveled woman in our midst.

Pop asked what all of us wanted to ask, "Why do you still live in San Bernardino?"

"Awwwh, James, you just don't know it, but this is Sunset Street and you will understand soon. This is one of those places called the 'thin places' of the earth, where heaven and earth collide."

My parents didn't understand but listened to Ms. Washington.

"Sunset Street has a rhythm like the flow of a river, I call it my little bit of paradise. Here I lay my head by the riverside." Then to our surprise, she started singing, "'I'm gonna lay down my heavy load, down by the riverside, down by the riverside.'"

Her voice was a medley of Whitney Houston and Aretha Franklin, or was it Helen Baylor and Nina Simone? It didn't matter because she was Emelia Washington, whose voice could free a demon from hell. I noticed that Adey was getting jittery, so I went to him.

"Hi, I'm Alero. My friends call me Allie."

"I'm Adey. A-d-e. My mom added the *y*."

"I like Adey!"

"Thank you! What does Alero mean?"

"It's actually Nigerian. My parents found it online and it means 'the ground is soft.'"

"I think is actually an Itsekiri word," he said.

"Yes, how did you know?"

He beamed a sheepish smile that said, "I know I'm smart but won't brag."

"How about your name? It's not common either."

"Well, you are now on Sunset Street, home to collective acceptance, individual grounding, and economic empowerment. All the families here are transplants from all over the world seeking a piece of the American dream. I stay because I've found acceptance and the United Nations."

"I don't even know what all that means."

"It means you will find Africans, West Indians, Brazilians, and Mexicans, married to African Americans or Caucasians, Native Americans, and each other, and all make this place the most diverse community. It's like a piece of the world in one place."

"Oh!"

"Yeah! My dad is Nigerian but he left us when I was five years old, so it's been my mother and me and all these people who treat me like their own."

"Sorry about your dad!"

"No need. I am forward-looking."

"You speak like an adult."

"It's an only child syndrome. I'm usually alone or in the company of adults. Kids bore me most times."

"What!"

"Sorry. You don't bore me."

"I'm sure we're about the same age?" I inquired.

"I'm twelve, soon turning thirteen," he said.

"I'm twelve."

"What does your name mean?" I returned to the original question.

"It means 'crown.'"

"How cool! Did your dad give you that name?"

"Yes, I think so." Adey was suddenly unsure. "I'm sure he did because Mom was born in Louisiana. She's Creole, her mother is Black and her father a Frenchman. She wouldn't have known about a Nigerian name or maybe she got it out of a magazine. Anyway, I remember Dad was present till I was five years old. I'm sure he named me," Adey responded confidently.

"Do you still keep in touch with your dad?"

"He is thousands of miles away, so I don't get to see him. I have great memories of him, though. I miss him a lot!"

At that moment I felt sad for Adey, a poor fatherless child. And without thinking, I said, "I will share my dad with you, but he's not a Nigerian so I hope you will manage." I grabbed his hands and we walked into the kitchen, where the adults were talking.

"Daddy!"

"Yes, Allie Pooh?"

"I told Adey that I will share my dad with him because his dad left for Nigeria and never came back."

Thinking back, it would have been awkward if not for my dad's response. He walked towards us and knelt on one knee to meet us at eye level.

"Young man, you are welcome to our home anytime. Remember no man can really replace your dad."

Adey nodded in agreement.

"Do me a favor too, young man."

"What is the favor, Mr. Smith?" Adey asked seriously.

"Take care of my daughter out there on the streets of San Bernardino."

Adey suddenly stood up straighter like a soldier and declared, "I will, sir! I will!"

I saw the mothers hide their laughter, but Pop and Adey seemed serious about their quid pro quo. That was the beginning of our relationship. Adey became my best friend. You've heard people talk about soul mates or perfect fits or better halves. I am not sure which phrase to use but I can only describe it as bottomless friendship. The type that cannot be exhausted and one can't seem to find when or where it started and it perpetually stays connected. It is what happened between Adey and me. We immediately became inseparable. We were in the same classes. Ms. Washington or

Momma took turns dropping us at school until we negotiated walking by ourselves. Adey and I would would walk back and forth to his house and then turn right back and walk to mine at any chance we got. Sometimes we simply talked to each other across the fence or read each other's lips. We even created our own language so others wouldn't understand us. I could sense him a mile away and liked the way he protected me on the walks back home. He even carried my schoolbag. It was difficult for me to introduce him to Shades and Eb because a part of me wanted to keep this private. I called him "my Adey," as if he were my possession. Shades and Ebony were reluctant to include him in our group until they saw how glued at the hips we were. Our Fridays turned to four of us unless Eb sent Adey away so the girls could discuss intimate issues like our periods. Adey didn't care for the four of us either. He endured my friends because he wanted to be with me. Our conversations were perpetual, and we had endless topics to discuss.

Chapter 4

The civil war made it to my house after a few years of living on Sunset Street. The devil himself found his way to our little piece of paradise and beguiled Pop and Momma. It started very subtle and wouldn't have been noticeable if you didn't have the privilege of living in the loving cocoon for most of your life. It was that Pop came home very late and Momma was no longer waiting up for him. It was the slightly rushed manner they now spoke to each other. Pop had to work more hours to keep up with the mortgage payment and the two cars parked in the garage. The house thermostat was adjusted to battleground degrees. First, there was silence, then a barrage of accusations flying from Pop to Momma and then from Momma to Pop until they forgot that I was in the house.

The truth is I never knew what they were fighting about, or I considered what they were fussing about to be not so important. Imagine the big fuss Momma made because Pop was too tired to eat the food she'd made for him. How could you punish a man for not eating? From my purview, it was up to his stomach and he would eat if he was hungry but Momma wasn't having it. She read him the riot act and came to fight with guns blazing. Pop ran out of his patience and started responding and the war was on in full force.

I would lock myself in the room, hoping to find protection within the four walls, but I felt safer scurrying to Adey's house and lying in his bed. Oh yes, Adey and I shared the same bed and never as much as kissed. We would simply lie there and talk and dream and solve life issues. I would tell him how miserable my life had become, and he would listen. If I cried, he would cry as we lay face up in the bed, not looking at each other but with his right hand holding my left hand tightly.

"Adey, I'm scared."

"The whole neighborhood can hear the fights."

"It is so embarrassing. I wish I could live in your house. Your mom is never home."

"It's lonely here, Allie Pooh," as he had taken to calling me.

We also learned silence in Adey's bed. It was the only place we ran out of words; after some time, it would get quiet as each of us got lost in thoughts. We still held hands but exchanged no words. I think it was then we learned to pick up each other's signals. Adey would know exactly when I was channeling him and would appear, and we kept this telepathic relationship our very own secret. We communicated in silence because the noise around us strangled our voices. I knew when his mom came home intoxicated or too tired to deal with him. I knew when he missed his dad and when he was focused on a test. Adey was competitive but not with me. He made sure that I studied so that we would place first and second in our class. I really didn't need him to help me study, but I enjoyed watching him take care of me. Eb and Shades said that boys liked to take care of girls and Adey filled my world.

Momma and Pop were becoming strangers. My mother was pregnant again and this time it looked like she would have the baby, as her belly grew noticeably. How they found time to make babies in between all the fighting eludes me. I secretly wished for a girl so I could have company in this duress. And another part of me was upset that they dared bring another child into this civil war. Adults were confusing. One day I had returned from Adey's house and Momma was home by herself with the door a little bit ajar. Momma must not have heard me because I noticed her taking off her clothes and I would have kept going to my room if not that I noticed something was off. She was taking off her stomach. My mother was wearing a pad and once she took it off, I could see that her stomach was as flat as mine. It felt like a grenade had been thrown into my chest, so I quickly ran out of the house and slid into Adey's bed. He knew I didn't want to talk so he just sat and watched me wrestle the demons in my head. *Does Pop know? How is she planning to explain after nine months? What has happened to my family?* I didn't know what to do. I finally vomited it all out on Adey and he sat there in a daze. We weren't equipped to handle these adult issues. Adey's mom chose that moment to arrive home drunk. Thankfully she was dropped off by a handsome guy. It looked like she drank when she wasn't on tour, as if to drown her ordinary reality until the next gig. Adey shut the door and turned off the lights, which made her walk past his door straight to her room. Once she shut her door, he turned the lights back on.

"Marry me!" Adey suddenly asked.

My heart skipped for joy and I knew that was what I wanted above anything else, but I said, "What do you mean marry me? You can't marry me."

"Why not?"

"We are not old enough."

"That's a made-up law. We can marry here and now in this room. We don't need a priest or church or anything just you and me against this crazy world."

"Okay, I will marry you, but you must ask me correctly and you need a ring, which you don't have."

"Wait!" Adey walked towards his desk and pulled out a ring that looked like an actual ring.

"Adey, where did you get that?"

"My grandmother gave it to me when we stayed with her in Louisiana. It's a family heirloom that I'm supposed to give to my wife."

"Oh, Adey, that's going too far. You should give that to your real wife when you are older."

"No, you will be my real wife. So be still and let me propose."

Adey knelt on both knees and held my hands, "Alero Smith, will you please marry me?"

"Yes!" I nodded.

The ring was a little big, so I took my necklace off and added the ring to it. I wore that ring every single day. And so we had another secret. We were our own family, a shelter from the war zone created by the adults around us.

Maybe Pop had walked in on Momma too, but I found them yelling about fake babies when I returned home.

"How could you do this to me?" Pop asked.

"I didn't do anything to you. I wanted to get your attention."

"You wanted to get my attention by faking a pregnancy?"

"Well!"

Pop turned around, grabbed his keys, and walked out of the house. I announced myself but Momma had gone into her bedroom and slammed the door. I was determined to be happy on my first day of marriage, so I slid in my bed and thought of my husband.

I don't know what happened to Momma and Pop, who had been so loving just a few years ago. I couldn't understand why Ms. Washington would have a child and let him basically parent himself or how my parents forgot about me in their battles.

It seemed Momma had committed an unpardonable sin. The pastor preached about sins that the good Lord couldn't forgive. I was always curious about which sin would tilt the scale of forgiveness to become unforgivable, but whatever it was had found its way to Pop and Momma on Sunset Street. Pop no longer cared to stay or eat at home. He arrived late and left very early. He still called me Allie Pooh and tried to laugh with me, but that was obliterated as soon as Momma showed up. They barely spoke to each other. Then one day, Sunset Street almost burned down. The sound of sirens cut through the silence on a Friday night. The house alarm was going off and Pop wasn't yet home. The house was filling up with smoke as we were the closest to the hillside. Momma woke me from sleep.

"Get up, Allie. Put on your robe and slippers, the hill is on fire. We are not safe."

I did as she told. On the way out, I asked where Pop was, and she simply shrugged.

Firefighters were in our homes by now, rushing us out. Part of the back of the house had already caught on fire. The fire had jumped from the hill to our trees in the back and now hoses were being strewn through our home. The entire street was now being evacuated. Adey and Ms. Washington were waiting with us. If the firefighters couldn't contain the fire, we would not be allowed home tonight. We all prayed and kept vigil. We all saw Pop running towards us. He ran like a man possessed, looking for us, and made his way to us. He scooped Momma and me into a hug and held us there. Momma started crying and I was getting embarrassed.

Could she wait till we got home, I thought. It was a wail uttered from a pained soul. Then she fell to her knees and Pop knelt with her, with fire blazing the surrounding hills.

I heard her say, "I was pregnant, James. I was pregnant but I miscarried two weeks ago. I am so tired of losing my babies."

"I am so sorry, baby. Why didn't you tell me?"

"You weren't there. You are no longer here with me. You've left me."

Then Pop held her close and I saw tears rolling down his face.

"Forgive me, Tolah. Forgive me," he whispered.

Adey and I saw redemption on Sunset Street. Right in the presence of a raging fire around us and inside our home.

We were told not to return. Ms. Washington swooped in and told us we were staying in Beverly Hills for the night.

Once we were set up in our luxurious suite, all courtesy of Ms. Washington, I heard Momma say, "Don't lose your soul because of work, James."

"It won't be forever, Tolah. I promise. Please bear with me. I love you."

He kissed her and Momma kissed him, and they kissed for a few minutes. I was afraid to come out of my hiding because I didn't want this moment to end. But Pop turned and said, "Allie Pooh, come out here."

I was caught. I went into the living room. Pop sat on a recliner and asked Momma to sit on his lap. He then asked me to come and sit on the other leg.

"Allie Pooh, I am so sorry for all the craziness I've caused. It is my job to love, guide, and protect. I'm sorry I've been gone so much. I'm sorry you had to endure all the fights. I only hope you and Momma can forgive me. I promise that when I'm home, it will be us just being family again and not fighting so much.

"You know Momma is the best thing in my life. I couldn't do half of what I do without her."

I nodded. "Yes!"

"I'm glad you agree," he said, and we all laughed.

"I am sorry!" Pop said again.

"I forgive you, Pop."

"Thank you," he said.

"I forgive you, James. Forgive me too. Let's circle it out."

"What does that mean?"

"Our cocoon of love hug! Come on, get in here."

We all cried and crawled right back into our love cocoon.

The pregnancy and the fire expunged evil from our house and once again Pop and Momma and I were back to loving on each other. People stopped by on Saturdays and Friday evenings to shoot the breeze. I was happy with Momma and Pop and I was happy with Adey.

Chapter 5

I was excited for the summer because we were free of homework and schedules. It was in the summers that I was allowed to take the bus 26 during the week to see Eb and Shades, who had concluded that Adey and I were dating. Everyone thought we were dating but we were so much stronger than that. How could I describe the tie that wrapped Adey and me in a bow? Adey and I were hewn out of the same earth and the Almighty breathed and sent us to the earth to find each other. He was everything. My soul double. My twin. My laughter. A few months after Adey gave me the ring, we had decided that we wouldn't label our relationship. We would love each other without rules. We never introduced each other as boyfriend or girlfriend. He was simply my Adey and I was his Allie Pooh. We were observers of the wreckage dating left in its wake as our friends at school were constantly breaking up. It didn't help that Ms. Washington kept chasing elusive love, men who promised to love but eventually swindled her. The Jordans down the street had already gotten a divorce and the Johnsons' daddy had simply walked out of the house and never come back. We swore to be together for life.

Summer before high school was a blast because Momma and Ms. Washington planned a trip with Eb and Shades's moms. Momma had the idea to take me on a road trip to Yosemite and San Francisco, about an eight-hour drive from San Bernardino. She, however, decided to make it a communal trip for my friends and their families. We were all so excited. Pop and Eb's stepdad, George would take turns driving the van. Ms. Washington took care of the accommodations as she said she knew how to get the best bargains and she did. We stayed in four- and five-star hotels with names I'd only seen in magazines. My mother was the Magellan, the great navigator who had printed all the directions and purchased books about exploring off the beaten path. Eb and Shades's moms oversaw provisions, loading the van with 99 cents store junk food. It looked like they'd raided the entire store. Our house was the departure point because Pop oversaw renting the van. Momma and Pop were all smiles, hugging and kissing like teenagers.

"Stop it, Momma and Pop." I screamed for them to stop embarrassing me, but they ignored me.

"Put on some music," Ms. Washington yelled.

"Not before we say a word of prayer," Momma said.

I thought to myself, *Oh now you remember prayer!* still embarrassed by the public display of affection. We were faithful Christians who went to church every Sunday. No matter how bad it got during the week in our neighborhood, I could always count on everyone taking the Sunday outing. Everyone shined their cars, put on their Sunday best, and rode to their respective church. We still worshipped at the Church of God in Christ, along with Ms. Washington and Eb and Shades's parents. Sunday was a day of fellowship, of laying down the weapons of war and forcing marriages into civilized suits for the sake of the Lord. I learned that there was something about Sunday to tame a marriage. It simply sucked the devil out of it for that day. All the warring couples got into their cars, put on their best faces, and drove to church to sit in pews to listen to therapeutic messages, which gave them the impetus for survival. It would last till the next Sunday. It was our seven days' shot.

In the van, Momma said, "Let us pray." We bowed our heads while Pop talked to God about each of us. He thanked him for providing the funds for the trip, for supplying all our needs, and then some. He asked for protection along the way and for Johnny, Eb's brother, who'd made the trip from Arizona, where he lived with his mom, to join us on this trip. He was about our age. Pop called everyone by name and even asked that Ms. Washington find a man who would bring her joy and travel the world with her. That got everyone giggling but Pop was serious. He prayed that the Lord would keep the men in their families, so they didn't lose their place. Pop gave the Lord a laundry list until Momma opened one eye to gauge if he was rounding up or just starting. I think she decided he was just getting started. Finally, Ms. Washington interrupted him with a loud amen and we all busted out laughing. Even the Lord has a sense of humor.

Adey sat next to the window, then I sat next to him and Ebony and Shade sat on the other seat next to me while Johnny sat in the row ahead with the adults. We talked, sang, danced, and used the restroom each time they stopped to purchase gasoline. The sound of laughter was healing. The sound of friendship was intoxicating. It was earth's way of preparing us for the next adventure if we survived this summer.

Adey held my hand in the van. He had never done that publicly before. I looked at him. Smiled and held his hand tighter. We didn't exchange a word. He listened as the girls and I discussed the latest dance moves, which Shades and Eb decided to demonstrate until Pop yelled for them to sit down. I saw Johnny give Shades a look and I made note of it for our next Friday gathering.

Yosemite National Park, on the western slopes of Central California's Sierra Nevada mountain range, was 1,200 square miles of breathtaking beauty, filled with granite walls, towering sequoias, and incredible waterfalls that draw millions of visitors each year. We arrived at the Ahwahnee Hotel at about ten in the morning. The moms hadn't wanted to camp. I was glad because we would have a decent place to sleep after hiking. We spent two days in the breathtaking park. We started our tour at Yosemite Valley and Cathedral Peak. When going through Yosemite Valley, we stopped to see El Capitan, Half Dome, and Inspiration Point. We visited the 2,425-foot Yosemite Falls. We lunched at the Yosemite Lodge before driving to a higher altitude and to a less-traveled part of the park, which Momma loved. We stopped in the groves of giant sequoia and saw some of the world's largest living organisms. We took pictures; standing beside the trees showed us just how insignificant human beings were in comparison to the majesty of nature. We stood by the Wawona Tree, otherwise known as the Fallen Tunnel Tree, a popular and impressive attraction. The story was that a hole had been carved out of the trunk in 1881 to let carriages, and eventually cars, drive through it. I imagined how the tree must have felt being invaded by cars and becoming a tourist attraction. This two-thousand-year-old tree became the centerpiece of our photographs, and whenever Pop set up his camera, the clicks didn't stop. We enjoyed the fresh Yosemite air before heading to San Francisco.

San Francisco was magical. Although hotels were exorbitant, Ms. Washington was able to book us into the Hilton at Union Square, perfect because we were close to the cable cars, which was a treat for us kids. My parents liked that it was close to Fisherman's Wharf and the shops of Pier 39. We walked the Golden Gate Bridge. It was here that Johnny came out of his shell. He simply became the funniest tour guide. He'd visited with his mom before, so it was a good time to show off. I guessed it was all for Shades. I smiled and looked at Adey, who nodded. I loved the way we could communicate without words. For the next three days, we toured San Francisco, including the Palace of Fine Arts, a Roman-style remnant of the 1915 Panama-Pacific International Exposition. We saw its outdoor rotunda and lagoon, which Ms. Washington fancied by the way she was taking pictures.

We tried to book a ferry to the former federal prison on Alcatraz Island, which had been home to some of the worst criminals in the US. The dads were not interested in going. Pop said he'd never been inside a jail and didn't intend to start in San Francisco so Alcatraz was canceled. We spent a lot of time at Fisherman's Wharf, Pier 39, and Ghirardelli Square. On one of the days, Momma insisted we visit the Exploratorium. We loved it. To us, it was a place for creativity and nerdiness. A citadel of learning, a place where the classroom came alive. We were like kids in a candy store. We stepped inside a tornado, turned upside down in a curved mirror, walked on a fog bridge, and explored several other hands-on exhibits.

The last day was a shopping day and we spent it in Haight-Ashbury. Momma and the other women had a plethora of lists to check off. I was simply glad to be in another world away from the known. The city felt like a hippie town with Victorian houses, anarchist bookstores, piercing salons, and funky clothing shops. We found just about anything in those shops, from hardware to punk gear and fishnets to upscale vintage clothes. We meandered towards Amoeba Records.

Finally, it was time to return home. We piled into the van at ten. For some reason, Eb's stepdad, had won the argument to drive at night. I say that he won because I could tell that Pop was not convinced. Within two hours we were all asleep except for Pop, who stayed up with Eb's stepdad.

However, the night was shattered by a screech. Pop was screaming, "George! George, take your foot off the brake!"

It must have started raining while we were asleep. It was not supposed to rain, but meteorology is not an exact science. I couldn't think because everyone was now screaming. It seemed the car was being carried by a strange force and we were facing oncoming traffic. A fourteen-wheeler couldn't stop in time, slammed into us, and dragged us a few yards before stopping. The last thing that I remember was that my head was slammed against some metal and I was wedged between something because I could move my head. I was in a pool of blood and couldn't talk. Then everything went dark.

Chapter 6

I was in a coma for weeks. When my eyes finally opened, I was in a hospital bed surrounded by strangers. It hurt to open my eyes, so I shut them again and found it difficult to lift even a finger. I heard a woman scream for a nurse and a couple came rushing in.

"She blinked! I saw it."

"She also moved her finger," I heard a man say.

I wondered if they didn't know that I could hear them. I tried to open my eyes again and one of the younger girls yelled, "She's opened them again!"

One of the nurses said, "Alero, nod your head if you can hear me."

I nodded and the whole room screamed. I could hear "Thank you, Jesus!" from the man who was holding my hand.

A woman who introduced herself as Dr. Suta started talking to me.

"Alero, you have been in a coma for two weeks. You sustained a head injury that caused your brain to swell and bleed, which is why your body shut down, to protect itself and allow the brain to heal from the severe swelling and internal bleeding. You also sustained some deep cuts on your leg and lost a bit of blood, but you will be fine."

I was struggling to understand this doctor because I couldn't remember anything. I was trying to recall but couldn't remember anything.

Dr. Suta must have noticed my confusion because she asked, "Alero, do you remember what happened?"

I said no faintly, but I don't think she heard me, so I moved my head side to side.

"Without moving your head, I want you to look at those in front of you." At that point, the man who was holding my hand and the woman next to me both stood in front of me, but I didn't recognize them. My confusion must have shown on my face.

"Hello, Allie Pooh, I'm your dad and I love you so much!" the tall man said.

The woman held on to him with tears rolling down her face.

"Allie, I'm your momma! I've been waiting for you to come back to me."

I wanted to tell these two how sorry I was to have put them through such trouble because they looked like they were suffering.

Then two young ladies came up to me.

"I am Ebony and this is Shade, but we call her Shades. You call me Eb, by the way." She started to cry too.

My head was starting to hurt so I closed my eyes.

There were a few other people in the room who kept coming up to me, but I couldn't remember any of them. I heard someone ask, "Where is Adey?"

"His mom dragged him to get something to eat."

"I don't blame her. That boy needs to eat."

And I fell asleep. By the time I woke up, the doctor in the blue scrubs was no longer in the room, but it looked like everyone else was there. They had removed some of the bandages and I was able to freely move my head. Then I saw this dark-skinned boy who was talking to a light-skinned woman. I remembered that he hadn't been in the room before I fell asleep. I could remember everything that had happened before I went to sleep but nothing prior to the hospital. I saw that most of the people in the room, including my mom and dad, were asleep, except for the woman and that guy with his back towards me. At that moment, the light-skinned woman saw me staring at her and screamed my name, "Alero! She's up!"

Then the guy turned around and I knew him. Couldn't remember his name, except that I remembered that someone had called him Adey. I said, "Adey." And he ran over to my bed, fell on me, and started sobbing. And I found tears rolling from my face also. I didn't know why but I could feel his pain. I whispered, "It's okay."

Finally, someone got Adey off me and he ran out of the room.

My dad went to get the nurse, and the same doctor came back with him. "A lot of excitement for one day," she said to no one in particular.

"Hello, Alero, you remembered Adey?"

"Yes!" I nodded.

Someone yelled for Adey to come back and he walked in on cue. He was smiling and I smiled too.

I remembered him as someone important, but I couldn't remember the stories.

The doctor said, "Alero, your brain will remember when it's ready. Let's get you a bit more comfortable. But first I want everyone to go home except for Mom and Dad. The rest of you can leave." I was sad to see Adey leave.

My mom and dad spent the entire night talking to me and telling me stories of myself and our family. They told me that I had been born at Kaiser Permanente on La Cienega in Los Angeles and that I was a Christmas baby. I came into this world on the 23 of December and my mom brought me home in a Christmas stocking. I tried to remember everything they said. My dad said that I would be a junior in high school in the fall and that myself and Adey were top of the class. They told me that I was best friends with Adey even though he was a boy. I was told that Eb and Shades were like sisters to me because we'd known each other since we were in vitro. Our moms had been pregnant around the same time. Shades was a May baby; Ebony was born in August; and I was born in December. Each time my mom and dad built the story of my life, my brain was rearranging itself.

The next day was more fun because my brain was clearer. I couldn't remember my past, but I knew everyone who stepped into the room from the stories that I'd been told. My mom and dad were sent home by the doctors and Adey, who showed up at six in the morning, took my dad's place next to me. He told me what had happened, that Eb's stepdad had been a mess since the accident. Locked himself in a room and wouldn't go to work or out of the house. He told me that the car had hydroplaned and that no one else had sustained any injury but me. It seemed that my seat belt had malfunctioned.

"Allie Pooh, I knew there was no way you wouldn't have fastened your seat belt when the police alleged that. Eventually they found out that the seat belt on your side was malfunctioning and didn't lock all the way. The rental company knew this but rented the van anyway. I think your parents will sue." He held my hand while he was telling me these stories and I held his. It felt right.

Eb and Shades and their parents came that afternoon, except for George, Eb's stepdad. By this time, my mom and dad were back. Eb and Shades talked to me about our Friday girls' club and how I should get well soon so we could start back up.

"Nothing is the same without you, Allie!"

"I am so glad you are back from the dead."

"Did I die?"

"No, you didn't, but you might as well have."

"Ebony, stop!" her mom yelled.

I smiled because I liked these two, a perfect complement. Eb was hilarious and Shades was serious.

A man walked into the room and we all turned to see him. Immediately I heard him the memory of his voice in my head saying, *Get in the van, everyone! We have to go!*

I repeated it out loud, "Get in the van, everyone! We have to go!"

Everyone froze, especially Dad George. I knew his name, Dad George!

His frame in that doorway had unhinged my brain and suddenly everything came back. I remembered!

Chapter 7

My recovery was more drastic than expected. I was out of the hospital by the end of the week. I was back to calling my parents Momma and Pop and Dad George was out of the room, clean-shaven, and going back to work. The holiday was too short but quite memorable. Adey and I were joined at the hip after the accident and he was even more attentive than he had been before, if that was possible. It was also just the beginning of hand-holding for Adey and me. He would walk to my door in the morning, waiting for me to come out so we could walk to school together. We would hold hands instinctively and talk about everything under the sun.

We talked about school, the future, heaven, hell, the president, our mothers and fathers, the latest hot music, the homeless man near our houses, teachers, friends, our fears, and our hopes. One would think that we would have run out of things to talk about but that was not possible. Adey would even talk about his science assignments in detail and I would learn from him, then it was his turn to listen to my talk about historical figures and how the textbooks were skewed in their presentation of American history. There were also times when we would hold hands in silence. There were beautiful silent moments when words were inadequate, and we basked in silence. There were other times when the silence was different, those were the days when I knew that Adey was in a melancholy mood, which could usually be traced to his father. I wished deeply that he could meet with his father or find an exorcist to rid him of these demons.

But we would walk or sit in silence for hours until he was able to function again. Once I asked, "Would you like me to leave you when are quiet like this?"

He shook his head, "No, please stay. You calm me."

His response scared me, because I didn't want to have that type of effect on anyone. What happened if I really had to leave? Was Adey depending on me too much?

I shook my head and said, "Okay."

Later in the week we were back to talking. We'd also decided to remove all marriage talks and focus on our friendship.

"Adey!" I said in a dramatic tone.

"Yes," he responded. "This sounds serious."

"Remember how you said that I calm you?"

"Yes, you do," he reiterated.

"What would happen if I was not there to calm you?"

"What do you mean?" Adey got a bit agitated.

"Well, now that we're no longer married," I joked,what will happen when we both start dating and eventually get married?"

"Alero Smith, what are you talking about?" He always said my full name when he was cross with me. "No one is dating or getting married at this minute right? Personally, I'm not sure I will ever marry."

"Do we have to talk about this?"

"Yes, because I don't want you to suffer."

He thought about it for a moment and said, "I will think about you and that will calm me."

Then he got excited, "Yes! That's it! I will think about you like you are near me and it will calm me." I got so excited that we'd found a way to bring him back to life and that I would be a part of it.

Shades, Eb, Adey, and I were having a great sophomore year at San Gorgonio High School. Shades and Eb were transfer students so they had to be bused to school every day; we walked back to my house until they were picked up in the evenings. We were active members of the civic group and the Black Student Union. Adey joined the science clubs and I found my way to the debate team. Eb was dating Marshawn, who didn't seem to be interested in school. I wondered why he bothered to wear pants if all they did was fall below his undergarments. And I could not fathom why such a smart girl like Eb found Marshawn attractive. I thought the concept of opposites attracting was overrated and antithetical to healthy relationships. The way I saw it, if you were with someone diametrically opposed to you, then life would be about trying to view things from their perspective, and you could end up disliking what had attracted you in the first place. People liked themselves, so the closer someone resembled you, the easier it was to live with them. I thought we needed someone similar but just a little different. What did I know, I was just a teenager. But I liked Adey because even though we were different in some ways, we mostly liked the same things and wanted similar things in life. We were both philosophical about life. We wanted to make significant differences in our communities and dreamed of visiting Africa as adults.

Marshawn failed all his classes but they kept passing him to the next grade because he was the captain of the basketball team. He'd led his team to the national championships and won. Marshawn seemed to be the only one able to leave Eb speechless. It was like she had no brains when she was with him. She dumbed herself down to his level, talking gibberish. He could smooth-talk his way through anything, so I understood why Eb had fallen for this guy, and he was cute. He was eye candy and six foot six inches of mahogany Adonis. It was still annoying how she lost her smartness around him and hung on to every word he said.

Like I'd suspected during our summer trip, Johnny and Shades were also an item. The union irked Eb, and understandably so. Her initial reaction was, "Can't she find another guy?"

"Well I'm glad it's long distance. I mean they can't do much between here and Arizona, right?"

"Why my brother, though?" Eb asked, ignoring my question.

"Why not your brother? He's a good guy and cute," I teased. "Plus, I've heard it's always good to marry someone who you know, and their family matters."

"Are you sure that you're not a marriage counselor"''

"Pay me, then!"

"Well, I don't like it but there's nothing I can do. Shades is too much for him."

"Look who is talking! How about you and Marshawn?"

"Well, people think Marshawn is dumb, but the boy is so smart. You should hear the things he talks about."

"Then why not demonstrate that in his grades? Does he know that people talk about how dumb he is? Sorry, Eb."

"That is so dumb how people judge without knowing. Marshawn thinks he won't be cool if he starts getting good grades. Do you know that he took an AP lit test in tenth grade and got a four?"

"Are you serious?"

"Yes, he showed me the result. He did it just for the fun of it. I guess to demonstrate his own smartness."

"Tell Marshawn to man up! Step up, brother, there is no shame in smartness. He's currently adding to the false narratives of Black men."

"I know! Maybe someday he will realize he's okay in his own skin. There's no one to guide the boy. His momma is never home. His dad is in prison."

"Adey's mom is never home, and his dad is thousands of miles away, but you don't see him acting the fool." I was annoyed that she was making excuses for him.

"I am not making excuses for him, Allie! It simply makes me sad."

I saw tears roll down Eb's face and I was stumped. What in the world was happening when Eb, my feisty, no-one-dare-talk-to-me, headshaking, debate team winner was weeping because of a boy?

"Come here, girl!"

I held her tightly and she held me with all her being. The type of hug that spreads warmth right through your flesh into your blood cells and grabs ahold of your soul's tentacle, letting you know that you are not alone. On the vast precipice of the earth, with its colossal mountains and immense oceans, there was a space on Sunset Street where two young girls dared to shatter boundaries and unanswered questions, bridge divides between hopes and dreams, and merge into a sisterhood. Love conquers. No more words were necessary. Sisterhood had won the day. We waved goodbye as Eb got on her bus home.

Adey continued this conversation with me later. We'd discovered similar thought patterns through questions like, "What were you thinking about when . . ." As soon as the question was answered, the other person would yell, "Me too!" They were our soul checkpoints. Whenever we were not flowing at the same altitude, it usually meant we were fighting, or, as Adey called it, "out of sync."

"You know Ebony is on a fast track to being like my mom," Adey said, walking back from one of our Friday evenings.

"What do you mean?"

"Black women who subjugate their identity for male acceptance."

"Big word! 'Subjugate'!" I teased. Also, I wasn't sure I wanted to discuss Eb after the moment I'd had with her.

"It's not so big, you are in honors English," he challenged.

"All right! I used to not understand what she saw in Marshawn. I thought maybe she thought that there were not enough boys so she was holding on to this loser. But I must tell you, Adey, I had a conversation with Eb and I see things a bit differently now."

"Really! Please elucidate."

"I can't explain it, but she gets him and he's not as dumb as he presents. He is not dumb at all."

"I still think she might be suppressing her own brilliance to keep a man because of fear of being alone," Adey continued with his argument.

"Well stated!" I said, not wanting to debate this topic with him. But I could tell Adey still wanted to make his point until we agreed.

"Just like Mom. I wish she would own her brilliance and just be. Has it occurred to these women that maybe if they let go of the trashy men, they would make room for good ones?"

"Adey, I swear you're going to be a preacher! What do you know about destiny?"

"Don't you believe in destiny?"

"I'm not sure. I haven't really thought about that yet. Destiny as in my destination as a human being?"

"Yes, as in the way of life. Why are you here? Where are you going?"

"Nope, I don't think I've thought about that. I don't know."

I could tell Adey was disappointed, but he got over his shock that his Allie Pooh was without a destination.

"Allie, how will you know when you've reached your destination if you don't know where you're going? I think you should start thinking about it because I can't have my best friend floating in the world without a compass."

"Compass?"

"Well, I think purpose is your compass."

"How can you know your purpose at this age?" I prodded.

"My destiny is to love my family and live a good life in the service of my maker."

I was disappointed. "That's it?" I asked. "How about your science? You could change the world, you know?"

"I know I am brilliant and will be very good professionally."

"Talk about confidence, Adey!"

"But it's the truth. I plan to make a difference but the most important thing to me is family. I want to be the best husband and father; that to me is making a huge difference in life."

"I don't think about marriage at all. For me, it's not something I dream about. I guess it's something I'll do, but I certainly don't dream about being the best wife and stuff. I want to change the world by being a voice to the voiceless."

"Okay, I can see that." Adey nodded. "But why don't you think of being a wife?" he prodded.

"Because I can't marry you," I whispered. "And if you and I can't marry, I'm not interested in spending the rest of my life with anyone else. And I can't get happy about you making another girl happy."

Adey held my hands, "We made a pact, remember."

I pivoted because I wasn't comfortable with this conversation. "Well, obviously Eb's destiny seems to be tied to Marshawn for now. But I found out today that Marshawn is quite smart and doesn't want people to know. He got a four on an AP English literature examination."

"Are you kidding?"

"Nope!"

"The thought of that is dissonant."

We both had a lot to think about. Adey had just introduced another dimension into my life, destiny. What was I destined to do or who was I destined to be and who was I destined to do it with? Several questions were left floating in my mind.

Chapter 8

The years went by quickly and we were now in our senior year. Momma and Pop were still in marital bliss, flourishing. They traveled to watch Ms. Washington's group whenever they could, and Adey and I sometimes went with them. I looked forward to those three or four days of travel to a part of Europe when the Butterflies were playing. In four years, we had flown to various countries including United Kingdom, Germany, France, Brazil, and Australia. Adey and I were fixtures in each others lives. People assumed a lot about the two of us, but I saw him as a part of me, not as a dating option. Since I couldn't date myself, it would have been impossible to date Adey and I was quite sure he felt the same way. Plus, we'd made that pact. I met several guys that I asked Adey to assess before going on dates with them. Somehow Adey and I found fault with each guy. On the other hand, I begged Adey to date someone. He seemed oblivious to his appeal. He had a lot of girls who loved him because of his care and attentiveness. Sometimes I got jealous but then I remembered it was Adey and I should not be jealous. One time he finally took some girl out to lunch and walked her to her front door, where both could hear her parents screaming at each other.

"Douglass, why did you leave the milk carton out?" the girl's mom asked.

"Because I'm buying the damn milk, that's why."

"No, you are not! I'm working too! Half of the milk is mine and you can leave your half out but keep mine refrigerated!"

"Pour your half out then!" her husband hissed.

"You are so useless!" she screamed.

"Woman, who you are calling useless? I will tell you who is useless! Your mama is useless! Your daddy is useless! Your whole family is useless." The girl was so embarrassed. You could hear them screaming a mile away. The woman was screaming about her husband's drunk dad and "like father, like son" and his slow mother and useless siblings. She went into a litany of everything wrong with his family!

The dad yelled, "Why did you marry me then?"

She retorted and must have walked away. She won that round and lived to fight another.

The girl was so embarrassed but Adey made her comfortable, like it was no big deal. Adey could not wait to get out of there, though, and used it as a reason not to date anymore.

Great things were happening to our group of four in this final year of high school. Adey was valedictorian and I was salutatorian. He'd been accepted to Harvard, as was expected, and had been offered a full ride to UCLA and USC; Eb had admission offers from Hampton University, a historically black college, and UCLA; Shades had been accepted to UC Berkeley and UC Irvine; and I'd received offers from Yale and a full ride to UCLA and USC. Adey and I had planned to attend Harvard or Yale together and it had never occurred to us that we wouldn't get into the same one. The decisions were not easy; our parents didn't want any of us to leave California. Ms. Washington was beside herself with joy that her son had been accepted at Harvard. She seemed to be the only one surprised that he was smart enough for an Ivy League school. On the other hand, she didn't want him to leave because Adey had become her de facto "husband," the one who fixed everything at the house and managed finances. She was indeed conflicted about his moving so far away. But no one from our neighborhood rejected Harvard, so it was settled for him. I also insisted he go, like his dad before him.

My parents were enthused about Yale, but my mother was convinced that being so far away on the East Coast was not reasonable for my first degree. They'd convinced me that this would not my last degree but my first. I didn't want to attend Yale without Adey and figured I might as well be in California. Momma and Pop decided that I would remain at UCLA, under their watchful eyes. There was no other decision to be made. I accepted. Adey was interviewed by a local newspaper and he became a celebrity that summer. I was glad because for once, the light was shining on someone with book smarts! Eb accepted the offer from Hamptons instead of UCLA because she got a full ride that could not be ignored. She convinced her parents to accept the decision with the promise of coming home after each semester. Shades chose the University of California, Berkeley, which I was happy about because she remained in California. We both agreed to pledge Alpha Kappa Alpha, one of the oldest Black sororities in the nation. One of our youth teachers at church had dazzled us with stories of their community engagements and how she'd traveled all over the world in service of AKA's mission.

That summer was a tale of two cities, it was the best and worst of times. I was deeply saddened because I didn't want to spend four years away from Adey. What would he do without me? I'd realized that I didn't know how to live without him. He'd been my life barometer for almost a decade. Adey was feeling the same. We no longer held hands but sat together in silence for long hours. Now we could only stay in each other's room if the door was open. Although Adey was always home alone, we still adhered to the rule. We would lie down on the bed face up and stare into space.

Ms. Washington decided to throw a party for Adey the last week of August, before he left for Harvard. He would be the first of the four of us to leave that summer. It was a pool party and friends from school, church, and the neighborhood were invited. Basically, though, all three groups were really one and the same. It was an opportunity for us to reminisce on the last four years of high school before commencing the adult world of college. Ms. Washington invited all the neighbors and she and Momma held court. Ms. Washington was dressed in a white miniskirt and oversized magenta blouse while her best friend, Momma, was dressed in white leggings and an oversized turquoise blouse. They both looked like they were part of a band and not someone's mother. I smiled because these two had rubbed off on each other in great ways. Momma had influenced Ms. Washington to embrace her family life while Ms. Washington had impacted Momma's fashion sense.

There was enough food to feed an army. They kept bringing out loads of fried chicken, Jamaican patties, pizza, drinks, hot dogs, hamburgers,

Nigerian moin-moin, meat pies, and so on. Pop and Dad George barbecued. The punch was monitored by Shades's mom, so no one spiked it, and Eb's mom was the official dance chaperone. Nothing went unnoticed. Life was good. Eb and Marshawn made an entrance and Johnny and Shades couldn't keep their eyes off each other. Marshawn had grown on me and I needed to get used to him anyway because he'd signed with UCLA. He was indeed intelligent. He could hold conversations on so many topics. I'd finally asked him one day why he was hiding his light. He said that people like him needed a platform from which to speak. Basketball would allow him to create that platform. I was amazed. We all needed platforms. We really shouldn't judge a book by its cover.

Johnny and Shades were such a cute couple. Shades had selected Berkeley because Johnny would be attending Stanford and they would be close in proximity. The Latino and African mix of Shades's complexion complemented the Mexican and Black mix of Johnny. Johnny loved Shades and vice versa. They simply fit. Johnny's passion was to go into business and become wealthy. Well, Shades was the business tycoon of the three of us, so I could see how these two were meant to be together.

Eb, Shades, and I walked to the front of Adey's house. Eb, the most dramatic of the three of us, pulled us into a group hug and started crying. Shades and I began to weep. Not a funeral type of wailing or "I hurt my foot" tears. These were tears to be remembered, that we'd made it against the odds. The teacher who'd singled Eb out as a rebel or the time when Shades had almost been gang-raped and the split-second distraction that had saved her life or the time when my parents were hellions in the house and these girls had been my support. We had laughed and cried and yelled and dreamed and sat in silence together. Now we needed to step out to live the life we'd dreamed of. We embraced one more time and wiped each other's tears because we would need this moment when the walls of our cocoon came crashing down. We would remember the friendships on Sunset Street.

Then Shades did something that surprised Eb and me. I think she surprised herself. She said, "Let us pray." Shades prayed on our behalf and asked for God's guidance and protection. We all said amen.

Eb and I received cars for our high school graduation. Adey gave his car to Shades and that touched my heart. Shades's mom cried and prayed for Adey and his mother. Ms. Washington had supported the idea. Adey's generosity never ceased to amaze me, and it came to him so effortlessly. To him, there was no point keeping the car when he would be thousands of miles away. Shades needed it more. He gave it to her.

We returned to the pool party. Adey, Marshawn, Johnny, and most of the boys and dads were in the pool. The mothers and most of the girls didn't want their hair getting messed up so they stayed out. Eb, Shades, and I jumped in the pool, enjoying the hot California sun. Shades's mom was at the side of the pool ensuring that no shenanigans were taking place. But the girls were together and the boys kept to themselves anyway. It seemed we all wanted to share the homogenous union as our last hurrah. When we came out of the pool, we raced to Pop's BBQ pit and had hot dogs on a bun with all the trimmings. Michael Jackson's "Beat It" was blasting.

A few of our teachers stopped by and that was cool. They ate, danced, talked, laughed about classroom teenage shenanigans, and some even sipped some of Ms. Washington's exotic wine. The rest of the teenagers got high on Kool-Aid, sparkling cider, and punch. Neighbors who worked late stopped by to wish us well and tell us how proud they were of us. Our old neighbors from Little Africa, including Mother Harris, came to bid us farewell and rejoice with our parents. It was a reunion and farewell. It was a happy day.

People finally started to leave, and I think the last families to leave were Shades and Eb's families. Then it was my parents, myself, Ms. Washington, and Adey sitting in the living room reminiscing on the years spent at Sunset Street. Stories began with "remember the time when," and we were rolling in laughter with tears running down our faces. It was amazing. Then it was time to leave. Adey had to get ready to leave for Cambridge in the morning. I'm not sure where the boldness came from, but I heard myself say, "Momma and Pop, may I please spend the night with Adey?"

I could see that my parents were shocked at the question. They hesitated and before they could respond, Adey asked the impossible, "Mr. and Mrs. Smith, can Allie Pooh stay the night? Please before you say no, know that nothing will happen. Remember when you told me to take care of your daughter all those years ago, Mr. Smith?"

My father, speechless, nodded his head yes.

"Well I have done that, and I intend to keep that promise. Allie is safe with me. We have agreed to not date or get married. She is more than my best friend, but I don't have a name for it yet. I just want to spend the night hanging and talking. My mom is here to chaperone if possible. I will sleep on the couch in the living room if we sleep at all, but I will return your daughter to you safely in the morning."

I too was speechless!

Pop looked at Momma, who shrugged her shoulders as if she agreed.

What madness! Surely Pop would not stand for this.

Pop looked at the room slowly and at Ms. Washington, then at Adey.

"Young man, you have never given us any reason to doubt your integrity, however, I have been your age, so here is what I will agree to. You two can hang out under the watchful eyes of your mother and when you start getting sleepy, I want you to call me and I will walk over to get my daughter."

My mouth fell open! Pop was cool like that!

"Pop, thank you!" I whispered.

My parents left and Ms. Washington was still standing with her jaw open!

"Mom, you can close your mouth now," Adey teased.

"Oh my gosh!" I exhaled.

All of us started laughing at the same time. Then we couldn't stop laughing. We laughed and cried and laughed until the three of us sat on the floor and just stayed there. Then Adey moved closer to me on the floor, held my hands, and I gently laid my head on his shoulder. We were facing Ms. Washington and she smiled. We fell asleep and the next thing I knew, Ms. Washington woke us to call Pop. But we quickly jumped up and decided sleep wasn't important. I called Pop to tell him that we would probably be up all night.

Adey and I packed up his room. Well, I should say that I packed up his room because Adey apparently was useless when it came to packing. I fell on the bed around five in the morning and Adey fell next to me. We sat there facing the ceiling in silence. Then Adey said, "How am I going to cope?"

"How am I going to cope? You are leaving me!" I started to cry.

"Please don't cry," he said.

Then I cried some more.

"The next thing you will write me that you have a girlfriend and then I won't hear from you again."

Then he said, "It doesn't matter if the girl isn't you."

I didn't understand that statement and I was too sad to try to decipher it.

He held me tight and we stayed there without saying a word. There was no need for words. Our hearts did the talking. Silence spoke volumes.

Then we heard the knock on the door. It was Momma and Pop at exactly 6:00 a.m. Ms. Washington opened the door and Adey and I walked to the door.

"Did someone die during the night?" Pop tried to make light of what he sensed. "Don't you have a plane to catch, young man?" It had been decided that Pop would drive Ms. Washington and Adey to the airport, and he would leave from there to work. Invariably I couldn't go.

"Let's get this car loaded," Pop said.

Pop and Adey loaded the car and it was then we noticed Ms. Washington crying; Momma was comforting her. I went over and hugged her because I had a sense of what she was feeling. I had wondered why Momma had come over since she wasn't going to the airport but now I understood. She was there to comfort us. Momma! Always so thoughtful! The wind beneath my wings. Finally, Adey and Ms. Washington got in the car and we waved goodbye and Momma and I watched them drive off. Then the car stopped, and I wondered what Adey could have forgotten. I saw him get out of the car, running towards us, and my mind was trying to figure out what he'd left in the house. I had double- and triple-checked everything but when I saw his face, I knew. It was me. He ran straight towards me with tears rolling down his face and he hugged me and whispered, "Please don't let me go." I hugged him tightly and I was afraid. Finally, someone separated us, and Adey got in the car and was gone.

Fifteen Years Later

Chapter *9*

I went on to earn a PhD in Clinical Psychology from UCLA and a law degree from Stanford University. I started a family law practice that specialized in trauma and divorce. I was also a community organizer, dealing with the inequities of those in neighborhoods like the one I grew up in. Memories of my youth became exactly that—memories. Nothing was the way I'd envisioned it in my life. I got married. The happenings of life made me forget that Adey and I had not spoken in over a decade and that by itself was unbelievable.

Ebony and Shade were both maids of honor at my wedding. Ebony ended up marrying Marshawn and I must give it to the sister, who saw what was hidden from most of us. Marshawn played for the Lakers and had become a business maverick. He created sustainable platforms for wealth in Black communities. He had his own clothing line, housing investments, and a production company. Ebony and Marshawn lived in Hollywood Hills. It was the nineties and Black American television was booming: *The Fresh Prince of Bel-Air*, *Martin*, *The Cosby Show*, and many more are celebrating Black lives. Ebony was living her dream as a Hollywood actress in a popular television show.

Shade and Johnny were global investors who trained people to invest in properties. They sold me my first property in Ladera Heights, an affluent Black neighborhood in Los Angeles. Johnny and Shade ensured that we all bought houses, including Marshawn and Ebony. Their philosophy was that the way out of poverty was real estate. View

Park had been mostly white until the 1960s, when the Supreme Court desegregated homeownership in the area and affluent and educated Blacks started moving to the area. Of course, the white folks left as Blacks began to move in. Black entertainers who were not welcomed in places like Bel-Air or Malibu also found their way to Ladera Heights and View Park. People like Debbie Allen, Ray Charles, Tina and Ike Turner all called the areas around LH home.

The girls and I bought during the recession and so we got the homes for a lot less than they were worth a few years before but they were now worth much more than what we'd bought them for. One day, I received a call from Johnny that it was time to sell if we had no desire to live there. It looked like none of us wanted to keep living in LH, so we sold the homes and each one of us made at least $250,000 on the sale. Not bad for an investment of $25,000.

Ebony, Shade, and I spent a week together at least once a year. We looked forward to the week away and took turns deciding what to do for seven days. We'd visited several parts of the world, sauntering through London museums, sailing across Eastern Europe, spending the week on a Greek island, dinrking shots in Florence. We were devoted to this tradition and each took turns deciding where to visit.

We spent Valentine's Day weekend in Paris one year when none of our partners were available. But it wasn't all about globe-trotting, there was the year the girls came to my dorm in law school and turned it into a retreat. We ate takeout, watched old movies, drank wine, and sang along with Whitney Houston. It was during these trips that we reconnected and brought each other up to speed on our lives. The questions on the last trip had focused on my wedding.

"So where is Adey?" Shade asked.

"You ask that question each year," I responded. "He's not here."

"He is still in Boston. The rising star in neurosurgery. I follow everything about the brother. He is a who's who!" Ebony exclaimed.

"I can't believe you are marrying someone else. It doesn't make sense."

"You all know that we were never dating, and Richard is okay."

"'Okay' shouldn't be getting married!" Ebony retorted.

"Just 'okay'?" Shade questioned.

"He's more than okay. We get along and I think we will be fine."

There was a whirlwind of planning happening around me, yet I seemed to be numb. Somehow the marriage seed had grown into a plant that I didn't understand. Momma and Pop were still living happily ever after but their luck in love must have skipped a generation. They'd repurposed their lives as empty nesters into providing youth mentorship from the Sunset Street house. I was, however, too involved with my life to be a part of it. My fiancé's name was Richard, of mixed heritage, as his father was white and his mom African American. Richard had been a staple in my life since graduate school. He was a medical resident at UCLA when we met at a conference on campus. I was intrigued by his ambition and focus. He had dreams of establishing himself as a person of substance in the community. I was attracted to his intensity. Richard would drop by my apartment and we would talk about psychology, politics, and medicine. He simply kept coming and since I wasn't dating, I allowed him to keep coming. At one point, I decided to buy a ticket to Boston because I thought it was time for Adey and I to talk. I had so much to tell him because nothing in my life was clear. I got to Harvard and, as fate would have it, I saw a couple walking ahead of me and since I could pick out Adey with a blindfold on, I knew that it was him. I instinctively hid so as not to be noticed. It was Adey and a lady, who were clearly together in their laughter, conversation, and body language. The woman brushed something off his shirt and held his hand. Adey glanced back as if he'd recognized someone, but I stayed behind the wall until they were far gone. I called a cab, got back to the airport as quickly as I could. On the flight back I contemplated why I hadn't said anything. I was annoyed that seeing Adey with another lady had impacted me so much. Then I got angry at all the years he'd allowed to pass without so much as a word. I was upset at the work of the amygdala, registering my love for Adey as a template, which made it difficult for me to move on. I was mad at Adey for forgetting so easily. All the heart-to-heart talks; all the promises spoken and unspoken. Now he was loving someone else. My heart was pounding so loud I could hear it. I couldn't breathe. Someone had broken into my love garden and pulled out all the flowers, stepped on each plant, and left it broken. I was heartbroken. Before that day, I thought maybe there was hope for us but seeing how free they were together was a shock to my system. I'd thought he belonged to me, but the world said differently. I had the urge to write, so I penned a poem to Adey.

I wake up to you
Days filled with thoughts of you
Filling air in spaces unfurled
I want to be rid of you.
Toss you like an unfit garment
Wash in the ocean
Erasing all traces of love
But you stick like skin to bone
Yoked to me.

I returned to California and signed up to volunteer in Rwanda, a country reeling from the aftermath of the civil war. As a clinical psychologist and human rights attorney, I felt a pull toward Rwanda. I would write the mental health curriculum for Mercy Orphanage and train the women workers at Mercy in the use of mental health first aid. Once I landed in Kigali, I was picked up by two elderly women, one an American, called Mama Betty, and a Rwandan lady, called Mama Runi, short for Runihura. I was told it meant "one who smashes to bits." Imagine being reminded daily that you are a wrecking ball. I immediately felt at home in Rwanda. My room was barely furnished but I had a bed and a net to prevent mosquitoes. This was my first trip to Africa, and it was to the other side of the wilderness. I'd heard stories of the parties in Lagos and the hustle and bustle of the city. The highlife of Lagos, and the men who were willing to treat you like a queen. My Nigerian friends had never been to Rwanda, so I had to consult Google to get my bearing. There was something about this broken-down country that called to me like deep calling after deep. The Rwandan genocide, the genocide of the Tutsi, had left the country in a state of shock. The war killings had gone on for a hundred days and here I was just a couple of years after. The mark of war was evident, with disabled citizens with one limb or no limbs. Those whose eyes had been plucked out and were left to retell the stories of the dead.

I arrived at the orphanage, which was in the middle of nowhere. The story was told of how these children had been smuggled to this place in car trunks or in the middle of the night. Many had lost their lives on their way here but after the war, the children came pouring in. Mercy had been founded by Mama Betty and Runi. The place was mostly run by women and I was well received. The children had lost both parents and most relatives and had nothing left but this place. I found solace in their pain. I spent a month nursing them, pouring life back into as many children as I could. A girl named Habimana, "God exists," clung to me and I began to call her Shadow. Her name was a contradiction to me. A paradox of sorts. How could God exist in this seemingly God-forsaken place? Habi, as she was called, had been pulled from underneath piles of dead bodies of her family members. For some reason, she had not been crushed or suffocated to death. Maybe God existed for her personally. It was in Rwanda that I poured all the affectionI could muster into these orphans. I trained the staff and had Mama Runi help me translate the curriculum to Kinyarwanda. I hardly slept. I worked with the nurses and trained them to be mental health responders. There was peace in their surroundings but fear in their hearts. Nighttime was filled with shrill cries of nightmares. After about a week and a half there, I saw a reduction in those, and everyone complimented me, but it was the effort of the entire group. We were all part of this recovery. The night before I left, I walked around the compound in the darkness of night, the moon covered by dark clouds. I couldn't find God. I couldn't locate him among the death smell in Rwanda. I couldn't locate him near me. I couldn't find the one Momma and Pop spoke so intimately about. I couldn't find my own. I took my soul and buried it in the African soil. I wouldn't need it anymore. I was alone.

Chapter *10*

I returned to Los Angeles a changed woman. Nothing was different on the outside, but I was no longer crying or hurting or hoping. I was ready to live life without attaching my heart to another. A carefree kind of love that didn't expect much heart vibrations. I resumed my relationship with Richard, who started talking about marriage. It came as a shock to me because I didn't understand why he would take such a complacent union to the overdrive of marriage. We hadn't even kissed and there was really no desire on my part to do so. We continued to discuss marriage in the abstract. But it seemed that Richard had a timeline and marriage was next on the checklist. The idea began to grow on me. He seemed like a good guy. There really was nothing to stop us. He was a nice young man. We would be comfortable in terms of income. I thought we would make a good couple. I noticed that he became jealous quickly of other men around me and I was getting tired of him interrogating me about every single guy I spoke to. One day late on Saturday evening after another argument about the guy Martin, who lived next door, Richard simply said, "I should marry you."

"Is that a proposal?" I joked.

"Yes," he said. "Marry me!"

"Are you sure?" I asked.

"Yes, I am sure. Marry me?"

"Okay, I guess."

"It's settled then, you are now engaged to be my wife. I will get the ring soon enough."

He then turned around and left the apartment. I thought maybe I'd fabricated the whole scene and Richard hadn't been in my apartment and I hadn't agreed to marry a man who hadn't asked me to marry him but had told me to marry him. And there is indeed a difference.

I was in a daze. What had I just done?

But it wasn't a dream because Richard returned that evening and insisted we tell our parents. We called my parents and it was official. We went to my parents' house that weekend. Pop was his jovial self and Momma made a big lunch and I helped clear the table. We were both in the kitchen when she asked, "Darling girl, how are you?"

"I'm fine, Momma! I've been quite busy."

Then there was silence and she stared intently at me. I got scared and asked if she was all right.

"Yes, child, never been better. But this is not about me. Are you sure about this? This feels so sudden. I didn't even know you two were serious."

"Yes, Momma! I'm sure. What is there not to be sure of? Richard has been in my orbit for the past year. We practically do everything together, why not put a ring on it?"

"How come you've never introduced him to us until today?"

"I don't know. I'm sorry."

"It's okay, Allie Pooh," Pop joined Momma and me in the kitchen.

The truth is my stay in Rwanda had imprinted in me the transiency of life and the risk involved in loving someone who might be gone the next minute. It was safe to live a transactional life. I liked Richard enough to marry him. We got along and I knew that he cared about me. The decision to marry seemed like a natural next step for us. I was still not sure why I had not yet introduced him to my parents. I didn't say any of this but simply said, "I'm sorry, Pop."

"Listen, child, you make sure you marry him only if he makes your heart sing."

"How do you mean?"

"In my opinion, there's no point casting your lot with someone who can't activate the heart song. Each heart has a song that is only played by the right person. Like a key opens a lock."

"I don't want anyone to play my heart! Richard is fine," I said with all the "this conversation is over" tone that I could muster.

"Allie Pooh, anything less will be misery," Pop said, as he held my face in his hands.

"I'm getting married, you guys should please stop the lecture."

"Let's circle it out," Pop said. We hugged.

Our next stop would be Richard's parents' home in Napa. Dr. David and Dr. Claire Braithwaite lived in an antebellum home. I felt like I'd arrived in the old Savannah, Georgia. It was a property with beautiful gardens and fountains that could be viewed from the back veranda and the sunroom. There were Corinthian columns all around the home and spectacular designs. There was a feeling of history and to me it felt like straight out of *Architectural Digest*. The Braithwaites had recreated a period in American history and all they needed were slaves to complete the plot. There were Black and Brown domestic staff, including butlers, chefs, and housekeepers, in perfectly ironed checkered uniforms. A young Mexican boy took my suitcase to the guest room. The house was intimidating and the coldness palpable. Richard started acting strange as soon as we entered. He became cold and distant. He kept following his father and repeating almost everything he said. Pictures of the Braithwaites filled the walls. Great-grandfather Braithwaite had bought the land in Napa Valley and each generation had added to it, until it had grown to two hundred acres of vineyards. The Braithwaites were the owners of the Braithwaite Winery, one of the fine California wineries. Husband and wife were now Wall Street investors who had added to the acreage and oversaw the business. They were both medical doctors who'd traded their stethoscope to run the business. I was escorted upstairs to prepare for dinner and Richard wandered off to another part of the house with his parents. I heard them whispering as I walked upstairs and decided to ask Richard later what that was about.

I'd been told that homes had energy and this one was pulsating with negative vibes. My skin was crawling, and I had the strongest urge to escape from the house, but I decided to look out the window instead. The terrace offered views of the vineyards. The grounds were shaded by citrus, fig, and stately cypress trees. There were acres of olive trees, which I was sure were for their award-winning olive oil.

"How can a place so beautiful feel so creepy?" I asked no one in particular.

Dinner was served and we were led to a formal dining room, complete with timeless dark wood floors, regal and stately with noble furnishing. The hall was ornate, with classical beauty. The handcrafted table, with elegantly tasseled chairs, could seat at least twelve people. David and Claire sat at opposite ends of the table while Richard and I were seated at opposite ends in the middle. David was a burly, tall white man who seemed engrossed in his own thoughts. He was gruff and brisk, and the domestic help seemed to shudder at his presence. He had piercing blue eyes that dared me to look at him and I did exactly that. I stared right back at David until he averted his eyes. That was practice and years of training and working with various types of clients or the sheer weight of having grown up with Pop and Momma Smith. I wasn't scared of David one bit. Claire was a light-skinned, small-built African American woman who could have passed for white, and I had a feeling she'd done that at some point in her life. She relished her status in life and wore it like royalty. Her eyes were an almond color, like her Richard's.

I was soon told that conversations should wait till after the meal. A four-course meal was served without enough time to enjoy each dish before the young Black girl whisked it away and a Latino man placed another course in front of us. I wondered if the rush was, so we didn't taste the meal or if this was how "old money" ate. At the end of the meal, Claire asked that we all go to the tearoom in what clearly was an overdrawn Southern accent. The tearoom was more comfortable but the people in the room made it quite impossible to relax. Their discomfort was palpable, and I had the urge to run again. But then they started serving wine, which took the edge off a bit. Richard had yet to say a word to me or look in my direction. He was fixed to David's side.

"So, young lady, I heard you are a therapist?" Dr. David Braithwaite broke the silence.

"Yes, sir, I have a doctorate in psychology and a law degree."

"Did you attend the same school as Richard?"

"I'm a UCLA-trained psychologist and Stanford-trained attorney."

"Impressive," he responded. "Who do you work for?"

"I contract with hospitals and have a legal practice in Westwood."

"Very good," he said

By now we were all seated and there seemed to be nothing else to say.

"Allie," Claire said ever so gently.

"Yes, ma'am."

"You want to marry into this family?"

"I hope so," I said. Although I didn't like the insinuation of plotting to be a Braithwaite.

"Do you know who we are?" she queried.

"Only what Richard has told me and honestly that's not a lot," I said, throwing Richard a look, but he was not looking my way.

"Who are your parents?" she continued.

"Tolah and James Smith," I responded.

"What do they do?"

Her tone got the best of me and I angrily blurted out, "My mom is a schoolteacher and my dad owns a construction company. We live in San Bernardino, California. They created a wonderful home for me to thrive and they are the most wonderful parents anyone could have." I suddenly felt the urge to defend my upbringing.

They all stared at me as if I had milk on my face, but I didn't care. I was ready to leave, and they could keep their son, who was useless to me at this point. At that moment, a man in a suit walked in with a briefcase. He opened it slowly and took out some documents.

"Please sign these," he said.

"What are they?"

"This is a prenup agreement that protects Richard in case of a divorce."

"Are you kidding?" I started laughing and the laughter became uncontrollable.

Holding the papers, I asked, when I could control the laughter, "Richard, is this why you've been acting like a zombie ever since we walked in?"

I looked at all three of them and said, "So ya'll plan for a divorce before the marriage. Wow! The way of the rich! Lawyer! Give me a pen."

I was so angry, but I signed the prenup documents without reading them and walked out of the room. I went upstairs and gathered my overnight case. I heard Richard running after me, but it was too late. I really didn't want anything to do with the Braithwaites and I obviously did not want this man.

"Richard, please call me a taxi. I will not spend another minute in this house. You can have your ring! Wait I don't even have a ring" I screamed. "We are not engaged!"

His mother entered the room as I was yelling at Richard with a different attitude. She was apologetic.

"Oh, darling! So sorry we treated you this way. We are so sorry. I think we were just nervous. You know Richard is our only son. Please stay. Forgive us."

I looked up and saw this woman was in tears and a part of me melted. Maybe they really were just nervous. I paused and nodded okay.

The rest of the stay was very nice. Claire was a hoot. She could make a rock laugh and her laughter was contagious. David decided we should do the electric slide and Richard, who had two left feet, joined and it was hilarious. We laughed, drank more wine, and ate tiramisu. We talked about the wedding and confirmed the date in July was good timing for everyone. Right before we all got ready to retire, Claire took out a jewelry case and gave it to Richard.

Richard opened it and got on one knee.

"Allie, will you marry me?"

My jaw dropped at the size of the ring.

"Oh my gosh!" I exclaimed.

"Is that a yes?" Richard teased

"Yes!" I said, with all the bells in my head screaming no.

He put the ring on my left ring finger and said, "This belonged to my great-grandmother and has been in the family waiting on another Braithwaite wife."

"I am honored!" I responded.

I went to bed thinking about the transformation in the Braithwaites— the fun, the ring, and Richard.

Our drive home was light. Richard apologized again for his earlier behavior and I accepted his apology.

Chapter *11*

M omma and Pop were livid!
　　"Do you know what you signed?"
　　"No, Momma! Who cares?"
　　"Look at this girl!" Pop threw his hands up and paced up and down the living room. "All that money we spent sending you to the best schools didn't buy you an ounce of common sense!"

"But, Pop . . ."

"Don't 'but, Pop' me!" he snapped. "You were kidnapped in the middle of the night to some Godforsaken place and coerced into signing a contract by an attorney without your legal representative present. And you didn't even read it over!"

"Pop, I am an attorney!"

"Okay but in this situation, you were not one."

"Do you have a copy of the documents?" Momma interjected.

"No, Momma! It's a standard prenup and I'm sure it's about me not touching anything that predates the wedding."

"Call off the wedding!" Momma declared.

Surely Pop wouldn't be a part of something so reckless, I thought. And to my surprise, Pop said, "Yes! Cancel it! Marriage is difficult enough to go in with your hands tied."

"Pop, I can't believe you guys care so much about money!"

"Look at this foolish girl. It's not about money, my Allie Pooh," he said so softly, I was forced to listen. "It's not about money! It's about your life!

There is something not right about this family and I don't know what it is. It just feels a bit off."

Momma interjected, "My spirit doesn't agree with it."

Just then the doorbell rang, and I went to get the door.

"Ms. Washington! It's been a while." I was glad for the distraction.

"Come here, beautiful! Have you been avoiding me? Each time I see your parents, they inform me that you've just left."

"I'm sorry, Ms. Washington, I've been very busy."

"I heard we are planning a wedding."

"Yes, ma'am!"

"What a shame."

'Why do you say that, ma'am?"

"Because I thought you would be my daughter-in-law. I never once thought you and Adey would end up with other people."

"I'm sorry, ma'am. Maybe the universe had other plans for us."

"We believe in God, not the universe!" Pop was quick to correct any of what he called "new age influence on the church."

"Nothing to be sorry about. If that son of mine could have found his way to California, maybe there would have been hope but he's stuck in Harvard and looks like he's always pursuing something new. He's now completing a fellowship in some neuro something!" she explained.

"I have not heard from Adey in ages and he stopped responding to my letters a long time ago. I wish him well, though. He deserves everything he gets because he's worked so hard."

"We were talking about Allie calling off her wedding!" Momma interjected.

"What? Why?"

"The Braithwaites made her sign a prenup in the middle of the night."

"These rich folks are crazy," Ms. Washington retorted. She turned to me, "Baby, what you do that for? Did you at least read it?"

"No, I didn't read it, Ms. Washington! There was no point and it didn't matter!" I was getting upset.

"Like I said, my heart doesn't agree," Momma repeated.

"Really! Really! Your heart doesn't agree because I don't care about what he makes or that I signed a stupid piece of paper so I can have some peace with my in-laws? You should see how they treated me before and after signing. But I really don't care because I am not marrying them. The truth is that none of it matters anyway. I will marry Richard."

I said my bit and walked out of the house, leaving my parents and Ms. Washington astonished. I had never walked off from my parents, but this whole thing was stifling me. I couldn't breathe so I had to get some air. I seemed to be dissociated, watching myself take such a major decision that my heart said was wrong. I walked out of my parents' house because I knew that they were right. But why not put an end to this, then? Why was I marrying Richard? I felt lost.

I called my parents and Ms. Washington later to apologize and the wedding plans resumed. They said they were sorry and that they trusted me to make decisions about my own life. *Well, you probably shouldn't*, I thought.

I went for my run the next morning. From my house to Fox Hills Mall in Culver City was about eleven miles round trip. This usually took me about two and a half hours. I ran to Admiralty, way past Bali, and ran until I got to Jefferson, remembering to wave to my fellow runners. I got to Slauson Avenue and wondered that no one really rested in LA. Then I headed home through Ballona Creek and slowed down on Lincoln and walked the rest of the way home. Running allowed me to clear my head and get ready for my day. This morning, I had so many ants crawling in my brain that needed to be fumigated. Richard was a clone of his father and it was difficult to look at him and not see David. Something was going on with those two—Richard turned into a little boy around his father and suddenly this brilliant doctor couldn't move without his dad's permission. However, being away from them had been great because Richard was back to his normal self and the Braithwaites had even visited my parents. Claire had asked my parents if the neighborhood was safe. "Of course," Pop responded sarcastically, "we actually only get two break-ins daily." And Momma joined in, "Don't forget the murders every thirty minutes." Claire was mortified until Momma explained that it was a joke but by this time, Claire had jumped up and apologized that they had to leave for another function. Richard left with them.

Pop started a soliloquy about the savagery of internalized oppression. This was when the oppressed became the oppressor because they saw themselves at fault or through the eyes of the oppressor. There was no better example than Claire Braithwaite, who marginalized her own people and saw them as undeserving. I could see what Pop meant but I left before he got too serious. If Richard was an offspring of these two, how did he really see me? And why was he marrying me? Should I break it off? But then where would I be? I would have loved to talk to Adey about all this but he had not contacted me in years. Why didn't he check on me? That sucked on many levels. My heart was broken but should I say splintered! He'd been my life barometer, my yardstick, but he'd simply left like I didn't matter. This wedding must go on.

Chapter 12

W e had been longtime members of Bishop Charles E. Blake's church and had attended a local branch of the Church of God in Christ in San Bernardino. It was settled that the wedding would take place at the main West Angeles COGIC. It was a good choice since the Braithwaites were apparently fans of Bishop Blake. For some of these guests, this would be their first time on this side of town. The Smiths found satisfaction that the wedding of their daughter would shed a bit of light on the beauty of this part of Los Angeles.

Pop walked me down the aisle in a dress that Richard and his mother had selected. But I didn't care, it was only a dress. The whole event was surreal. Like an out-of-body experience. I didn't really believe that I was marrying Richard. I kept thinking that I would wake up and it would have all been a bad dream. I knew I was making a mistake, but we were so far gone that I couldn't stop it. *Why am I marrying Richard except for the fact he proposed?* I also didn't want to be a statistic. I was quite aware that almost sixty percent of Black women were never married. *That's astounding! How can that many women simply remain single? Is it because no one has popped the question? I'm doing this for all those sisters who would have said yes but didn't get asked. I said yes to the proposal, so marriage, here I come.*

Ms. Washington sat next to Momma and Pop, as she had become family, a sister of sorts to my parents. I expected Adey to be at the wedding. At least I hoped he would be. It was incomprehensible that I would not be sharing this important time of my life with him. Ebony and Shade were my maids of honor. They both looked gorgeous in pearl-pink A-line chiffon floor-length dresses with a beaded top. Both Richard's groomsmen had been handpicked by his father. None of Richard's close friends had made the cut and he'd said absolutely nothing. Those who stood beside him were Nick, son of the family attorney, and George, son of a business partner. I asked Richard about the weirdness of this and he said that was how it was done. Our wedding had to yield a return on investment, so all factors that could be manipulated by David got the Braithwaite treatment.

As Pop walked me towards Richard, I suddenly felt this urge to flee. My feet, however, were stuck, and I couldn't move. I stopped walking in the middle of "My Love," by Lionel Richie. That wasn't our song. We didn't have a song.

"Are you okay?" Pop asked.

"No." I shook my head. "I don't think I can do this."

"Well, we are here now, young lady. But you say the word and I will turn around."

Just then I saw Richard, pleading with me. He beckoned me to come with his hands. My legs were unglued, and I moved towards him in response. There was no turning back.

Everything was a blur from that point. I noticed that Richard hadn't gotten a haircut. Who got married without a haircut? I was sure there was a barber somewhere in Los Angeles who could have cut his hair. He was staring at me, but I couldn't look him in the eye. My eyes were glued to his hair. I noticed he had a few greys and wondered if he would dye them or leave them to multiply until he was silver haired. The next thing I heard, "I now pronounce you husband and wife!"

And at that moment I saw Adey slide into a seat in the back of the church. I don't even know how I noticed but I did. I had a sixth sense for Adey.

Now he comes! I thought.

That was the last time I saw him. I don't think he stayed more than a few minutes. There were no congratulations; there was no "I've been sick or locked up in a psych ward is the reason why I haven't been able to contact you."

Chapter *13*

Richard and I flew to Paris for our honeymoon. Richard was not interested in having sex, though. I had brought along sexy lingerie, but the wedding night didn't go as expected. I thought maybe he was waiting till the next day and still, nothing happened. When I asked him what the problem was, he said he was waiting for just the right time. On the third night of our honeymoon, I was woken by a drunken Richard!

"Wake up, Allie! Wake up!" He was shaking me hard.

The next thing I knew, he yanked off my nightgown and spread my legs apart, forcing himself on me.

"Wait, what are you doing? You are hurting me!" I screamed.

He held me down, acting like a maniac. His face was contorted.

He pulled down his pants halfway and thrust his penis inside me. It felt like hot coals in my vagina. The pain was excruciating, and he kept lurching until he was satiated. He rolled over and went to sleep.

The tears started slowly at first and then became a bit more uncontrollable. I had been violated by my husband. *Congratulations, Alero!* How did I get here? I'd saved my virginity all those years for this. It was snatched like in a nighttime break-in. I crawled into the bathroom, ran a bath, and sat in it. My sobs could be heard miles away, while on the other side of the door Richard snored.

Richard woke up the next day and continued as if nothing had happened. I was wide-eyed, waiting for him to say something or extend an apology. Maybe the drink had made him do it, but all I got was silence. We continued our tours like a happy couple. When I couldn't take it anymore, I moved closer to him on the double-decker French trolley so no one would hear me.

"You raped me!" I stated.

"Shhh, keep your voice down," he said

"I am as close to you as possible. No one can hear us! And if they hear, I don't care."

"I didn't rape you."

"What!"

"I didn't rape you! I'm your husband. We had sex, that was not rape."

"But you did! What do you call what you did?"

"I was having sex with my wife, who had been complaining about not having sex the past few days."

"Richard, we were supposed to make love. That was rape!"

"I wish you would stop saying that! I gave you what you wanted."

It was like talking to a brick wall. I left the conversation. Richard proceeded to rape me each night after that until it was time to leave for Los Angeles. It got better after the first time because I drifted to another place and left my body. Richard couldn't hurt me anymore and my body would heal. I would leave him as soon as I got to LA, or at least that's what I thought. By the time I got on the plane, I was sore, broken, and dejected. *Who is this monster that I married? What have I done? Who would believe this?*

When we got home, Richard played nice and apologized for how he'd hurt me. He woke me up one night and began to weep, crying for my forgiveness. I asked him why he'd done those things to me and he began to talk.

"Allie, I am so sorry to have hurt you the way I did. I am not sure I know how to make love without dominating."

"Is that what we call it, dominating?"

"Please hear me out. I was four years old and the only child. Mom and Dad worked all the time and I was left with the most wonderful nanny, Elizabeth. She did everything a mom should do, told me how wonderful I was and how I would be the best doctor in the world. She filled the void Mom and Dad left. There was a lot of fighting in the house and we didn't have many visitors except for my grandpa and grandma. The strangest things happened in the Braithwaite house. At night I would see my father leave his bedroom and Grandpa would enter. I thought maybe it was to calm my mother down after all the fights, then I could hear my mother crying in the middle of the night and making noises that made me drown my head in my pillow. A few minutes later, my father would enter the room and begin hitting my mom. One day they forgot to shut the door and I crept closer and I saw my dad beating her with a belt while having anal sex with her. He called her all types of names, whore, bitch, while my mother's face was shoved in a pillow. Something happened after that night because my father started leaving the door ajar and I would watch. One day he turned and looked at me while thrusting into my mom and smiled and, for some reason, I smiled back. Then Grandpa started leaving the door open and I would watch him do the same thing to my mother.

"One day instead of Grandpa going into my mom's room, he stopped by my room and said to me, 'Now, Richard, there is a reason why we Braithwaite men must stay together and today will begin your initiation. You must be brave.' I nodded my head yes.

"'Pull down your pants.' I hesitated.

"'Do you trust me?' he asked.

"I nodded.

"'Pull down your pants.' I complied.

"Grandpa pushed my face down on the bed and penetrated. Then he pulled his pants up and yelled for my father to come up.

"Dad walked into my room and saw my face in the bed with pants down.

"He rushed towards my grandfather as if to hit him, but Grandpa grabbed his hands and said, 'I did you a favor. You must make him one of us. Now finish what I've started.'

"My father sounded like a demon. He turned me to face him and his eyes were possessed. He was no longer the man who'd smiled at me. He flung me on the bed and proceeded to violate me. Somewhere in the house, I could hear my mother screeching, but she never came to rescue me. That began my initiation to the Braithwaite madness. The worst was when they made me rape my own mother while they both stood there and watched me do it. I hate all of them. I hate my mother, who is spineless, and my father and grandfather, who are evil. In all the craziness, Elizabeth would restore my faith in humanity. I would pray for the summers to be over so Elizabeth could return to our home. She had been my father's nanny but refused to retire. I awaited Elizabeth's return. When she came back after the first summer, she looked at me and told me to come to her. She set me on the bed and rubbed my back while singing a Spanish lullaby that I couldn't understand but it ripped my heart apart and I wept. She kept saying, 'It's okay! You will be okay Richard.'

"Unfortunately, my parents returned without warning and found Elizabeth singing to me and that was the last time. She was forced into retirement by my parents, who bought her a house and paid for all her children to attend college. She retired to Mexico.

"They destroyed my life. It is the reason I never wanted to get married, because I didn't want to expose any woman to this, but I was getting pressed to get married. Dad said we needed another woman, fresh blood. And when you showed up with your beautiful disposition, you reminded me of Elizabeth. I thought maybe there was a God and you had been sent to save me."

"You married me because I reminded you of your nanny?" I queried.

"Yes." He nodded.

He was weeping and I was weeping for very different reasons, I suppose. How could anyone do something so heinous to a child? And why was I married to him?

"You were only a child." I felt sorry for him.

"I am so sorry, Allie. Please forgive me. I will try to do better."

"One thing you need to know, Richard, I will never step inside your parents' house again. Please don't ask."

"Deal!"

"We also need to go to therapy and report them to the police!"

"I have no problem with therapy, but I can't share the things that I've shared with you with anyone. If you tell the police, I will deny it."

"It will be our secret till death do us part."

"Promise!" he said with intensity.

"Okay!" I nodded.

I felt like I could save him. I could help him become the person he was meant to be. Things returned to normal and Richard made time for therapy.

Chapter *14*

I was pregnant.

Pregnant and scared. I didn't want my child to be exposed to the genetic dysfunction of the Braithwaites, but Richard assured me that he was doing better and would not allow his dad and grandpa to be anywhere near my child.

My parents were elated. Their first grandchild and they couldn't stop purchasing nursery items. Then Richard said that we couldn't have my parents coming over while his couldn't and it made some sense so I told Momma and Pop that I was opening another office and wouldn't be at home as much. Momma wondered why I would make such a decision at six months pregnant. I started seeing them on Sundays at church. I sat next to them. I was usually by myself because Richard worked most weekends. It allowed me to have my parents to myself. We went to my parents' house for lunch after the church service. I treasured these Sundays. I hugged my parents more and they noticed.

"Pregnancy really agrees with you," Momma said.

I got choked up and gave both my parents hugs. "I just love you two. Never forget that."

"How can we forget when you slobber all over us?" Pop teased.

"No more of that crying. I don't want you getting my granddaughter depressed. Now please get something to eat and remember she comes first," Momma said.

"It's our grand*son*," Pop responded.

"Both of you stop it!" I smiled. "You will love the baby, period."

"We already do!" my parents said in unison.

As if on cue, Ms. Washington walked in right when Momma announced the food was ready. I began to wonder if these two had a way of communicating that we weren't aware of. Ms. Washington brought me more diapers in addition to the several hundred she'd already deposited in the nursery. She told me that I would thank her once I realized that babies went through diapers like pigs and dirt. I could never understand that correlation, but I'd learned not to bother my head with Washington-isms.

The summer of our third year of marriage flew by. Richard was attentive and loving. He would be finished with his fellowship in time for the baby's arrival and already had job offers. He wanted to practice as a neurosurgeon, but his parents were pressuring him to take over the wine business. I encouraged him to take a job at a UCLA medical center, ranked as one of the top hospitals in the nation. His parents relented when both sides agreed that he would work for five years and then take over the running of the US division of the winery.

On the day of delivery, the Braithwaites, my parents, and Ms. Washington were at Cedars-Sinai hospital. I was too tired to resist them. Richard was attentive and at 2:15 a.m., Caleb Braithwaite entered his world. He looked like me.

"I am so glad you look like your momma, since the beauty and brains run on my side of the family," I joked.

Everyone laughed and I took the baby back from Richard. The Braithwaites stood far away enough to ooh and aahh at the baby—"He's so beautiful!" Claire said from afar. Then they were all gone except for Momma, who refused to leave my side, and I was glad. She went home with me and cared for me so I could care for my child. I was so glad for her presence. Richard went back to work the next day.

One night, Momma sat on my bed rubbing my back while I nursed Caleb. She said, "Dear child, be careful."

I didn't understand what she meant since everything was all right with Richard and I, and Paris was a million years away. We hadn't had sex in a while because of the pregnancy and Richard working long hours. Come to think of it, it had been almost a year. After Paris, we'd been able to have consensual sex, but it was always rushed. It was over in seconds.

I didn't complain because I knew it was still a struggle for him. He still fought demons in that aspect. I was also more understanding because I understood trauma-induced behaviors.

I asked Momma again, "Why do you say that, Momma?"

"Nothing, it's intuition."

I had never doubted Momma's intuition ever since I was a kid and she'd told me my favorite teacher would leave before the end of the year and of course, Mrs. Jackson and her family relocated to Florida. Since then, when she told me about her intuition, I took it seriously. As a kid, though, I didn't call it intuition, I simply understood that Momma knew things most of us didn't know. I nodded my head and said, "Okay, Momma, I will be careful."

Then she grabbed my hands and said, "Promise you will call if you or the baby are in any kind of trouble."

"Momma, you are scaring me."

"Promise me," she insisted.

"I promise!"

"Also, I will be dropping by your house more frequently. Can I get a copy of your key, so I don't disturb you and the baby?"

"Momma, we don't have keys. You need the code." I gave it to her.

"Oh yes! I forgot. This is high-tech stuff."

"Yes, Momma."

"Please do not tell your husband you gave me the code."

"You know Bishop said we shouldn't keep secrets from our husbands."

"Well, Bishop ain't married to him."

I was silent. I didn't defend Richard.

By the time my mother left for home, I was a bit more settled and felt safer. Somehow, though I had not told her anything, she knew something was wrong with this marriage. In our daily life, there didn't seem much to complain about. It was a sense of foreboding that a shoe would drop soon. And not just any shoe, a colossal shoe that could trample all we'd tried to build on this fragile foundation. Caleb was a good baby, the light of my life. I didn't realize that a human being could be capable of such depth of love. It was as if a dead bulb in my heart had been lit, an incandescent light of love. Richard was in the habit of arriving home late and heading straight to Caleb's room to quickly say hello before coming to mine. I knew this because I had installed video cameras all over the house that only I had access to. I didn't trust Richard no matter how much I tried. Things seemed to be okay but I knew there weren't. A storm was brewing.

Chapter *15*

O n schedule, as agreed, Richard stopped practicing medicine and went into the winery business. I refused to move to Napa Valley, so Richard would shuttle back and forth from our home in Los Angeles. It started with daily flights, then progressed to staying there during the week and coming home on the weekends. Caleb was five years old. Richard wouldn't allow him to see my parents because I did the same to his parents. However, since Momma and Pop didn't know the story of Richard's family, it was impossible to keep Caleb from them. At first, there wasn't much difference in our lives because Richard was gone almost as much as he had been when he was a physician. But then I started noticing that he had become glitzy. He bought expensive cars and visited Las Vegas almost every weekend. The first luxury car he purchased was the Ferrari's entry-level Portofino. I wondered why he needed an almost 600-horsepower vehicle until l drove with him to Las Vegas and Richard drove like he was on a racetrack. Then came the Lamborghini and the Bentley and the Mercedes. There were only two parked at our house at a time, but I had no idea how many cars Richard owned. He picked up gambling and won more than he lost.

One Thursday, as usual, Momma picked up Caleb from school and he was excited to spend some time with his friends on Sunset Street. Caleb had created his own space there that was different from the one we offered him in our house. Richard was not expected home until the weekend, which is why I didn't make a fuss about Caleb staying longer with his grandparents. I looked forward to washing my hair, then crawling up on the living room sofa with a good book and a glass of wine.

But I heard him come in. *He shouldn't be home*, I thought with all the hair on my neck rising in discomfort. I heard Richard lock the door behind him while I was getting something from my closet. I quickly beelined to the bathroom and locked the door.

"Hello, Richard," I called out.

Silence.

I put on my pajamas, put my hair in a ponytail, and walked back to the room as calmly as I could.

I found Richard staring into space and once he saw me, his eyes glazed over like a possessed alien. The next thing I knew, he leapt forward and began to rain his fist on my body. He paused to yank my hair and used it to drag me across the room to the closet mirror, as if he wanted me to see him humiliating me.

"Where is my son?" he yelled.

"At my parents'."

"Did I not tell you that they weren't allowed to take him to their house if my parents can't do the same?"

The punches and kicks intensified, and he dragged me to the toilet, where he proceeded to dunk my face in the toilet bowl. I kept struggling to breathe but then when I thought it was over, he lifted my head so I could catch some air and then dunked it again and again until I was too exhausted to fight and waited for death. It was then Richard threw me against the wall and I fell to the ground. I would not beg him. He wanted me to cower and I would not do that.

"You simply don't listen! You make me do crazy things! Why did I have to find out from Mom and Dad that your mother picks him up on Thursdays!"

"How did they know?"

"They know everything, you idiot!" And he kicked me in the stomach again.

"Grab your things, we are going to Vegas!"

"I am not going anywhere!"

He pulled me by the hair and said, "You are going, or I will kill you and him!"

"Him who?"

"Caleb! He is a disaster waiting to happen." Richard started laughing. A sinister laugh. "You think you are protecting him from the Braithwaite curse? You are a fool. They will get to him. I told you to have a girl, but you had to have a boy! Now you are both going to die!"

"Please, Richard! Not my son! I will do anything. I will go to Vegas!"

"I knew you would see reason. Now get dressed and look gorgeous."

My head was pounding but I looked around and didn't see any blood, so I crawled into the bathroom. My face was bruised but it was nothing makeup couldn't cover up. I called Pop to keep Caleb and take him to school in the morning, but Momma got on the phone before I hung up.

"Why are we taking him to school tomorrow? You always take him."

"Richard bought us tickets for a show in Las Vegas and we leave tonight."

"Well, I don't like the sound of this. Be careful," she responded.

Richard pulled his Porsche in the driveway and yelled, "Let's go!"

I put my overnight bag in the back seat and sat in the front without looking at him. There was no conversation in the car as Richard drove. He was driving at excessive speed and I willed us to be pulled over by cops, but no such luck. We arrived in Vegas and Richard started pointing to clubs and hotels owned by his family. We pulled into one and the valet greeted us.

"Welcome, Mr. Braithwaite!"

And again, "Welcome, Mr. Braithwaite!" as people kept coming out to greet him.

As we entered the hotel, women walked up to Richard, wanting to say something to him or touch him or kiss him.

"Richard, love! I miss you," said a red-haired woman in a mini skirt and with her boobs hanging out.

"How are you, darling?" asked another.

We walked into a high roller private room and Richard told me to sit at a nearby table. Two ladies came out and sat on either side of Richard. Touching his neck and hair and kissing him. I wanted to leave but he turned around and ordered me to stay there. I remembered Caleb and stayed. This went on for a while until he lost $100K. It was then he yelled,

"Let's go!" I followed him, thinking we were going to the hotel, but he bellowed for his car to be brought. We got in and he sped out.

"Where are we going?" I asked.

"Back home! You are nothing but bad luck. I have never lost that much money ever! You are bad luck! Bad luck!" He kept hitting the steering wheel. I closed my eyes to block him out but then I heard the car stop. I looked out and it was stretches and stretches of nothing.

"Do we have a flat?"

"No."

"Get out of my car!"

"What do you mean, Richard? It's dangerous."

"Get out of my car. You can walk home or get a lift. You are driving me nuts. I cannot stand the sight of you. I hate you! Get out!"

I got out of the car without saying another word and Richard sped off.

I began to walk, hoping to get to a call box but there was nothing in sight. I was barefoot by now because I found that it was easier to walk without shoes. I got off the shoulder and walked on the road because it was smoother. Cars zoomed pass me and honked for me to get out of the way. I felt nothing. No tears. No fear. I concentrated on walking. I wondered how Richard could drive at such speed and not get pulled over once while people from the neighborhood I grew up in got stopped by the police at high frequency for driving nice cars or any other fabricated reason. For some reason, I was enjoying this walk. I was glad not to be in the car with a madman. I would walk twenty thousand miles just to get away from him. I must have been lost in my own thoughts, but suddenly I heard a car park behind me.

"Where do you think you're going?" Richard yelled.

"Home!"

"Get in the car, moron."

I kept walking. I heard Richard catching up with me. He grabbed my hands and pulled me to the car. Nothing could stop him tonight if he planned to kill me.

Caleb came home the next day and I did my best to be his mother. I needed strength to protect him. We settled into another season of normalcy because Richard was gone the next morning and didn't return for another couple of weeks. He returned in a better mood. He played golf with Caleb.

A few weeks later, I got summoned by Richard again.

"Call the nanny to watch Caleb. We are going to Vegas at four."

I paused without answering.

"It is not a suggestion," he yelled.

"Okay." I looked at the time and it was one, so I had enough time to ask Momma to pick up Caleb and take him to her house.

"Hello, Momma."

"Hey, Allie."

"Momma, can you pick up Caleb and have him spend the night with you and Pop?"

"Of course, but where are you going?"

"Richard called and wants to take me to Vegas."

"Again!"

"Yes, Momma."

"In the middle of the week. People wait till the weekend to go to Vegas. He can't keep upending your schedule because he doesn't have a job."

"He has a job, Momma. He runs the business now." And I hated having to make excuses for him.

"Well he seems to have too much time on his hands, however, he should know that you have a business to run too. Allie, please be careful."

I said goodbye to Momma. Richard pulled up in a Maserati. I put my overnight case in the back and climbed into the front seat. In the good times, he would have opened the door for me. We drove to Vegas in silence. We were escorted to the high roller private room, where Richard won a stunning amount of money. We then went to one of his clubs, where the girls swarmed around him like bees. He was high on life and alcohol. He told me not to move from my seat while he pulled one of the girls to the dance floor. They started making out on the dance floor. I'd had enough, so I walked over to him, tapped him on the shoulder, and whispered, "Please take me home."

Richard pulled me by the ears and dragged me through the nightclub while people watched in silence. He dragged me into a room, locked the door, and I knew that I'd awakened the demons and that they would come for me tonight.

I instinctively balled up so he wouldn't hit my face, but Richard had something different in mind.

"Stand up," he yelled.

I got up slowly, still covering my face.

"Put your hands to your side."

I complied.

Richard came closer and began to rip my blouse until my bra was exposed.

I watched in shock and didn't know what to say. Then he said, "Let's go."

"Like this?" I asked.

"But of course, you piece of shit!"

I shook my head in disbelief. There was no bottom with this man. I had fallen into a bottomless pit.

Richard picked up a sturdy decorative cube from the table and said, "Black slut, I will break this on your head if you don't move!"

I followed him like a used-up hooker without even bothering to cover myself.

I sat at the table as I was ordered and watched Richard return to the dance floor with another woman. But I couldn't cry. I had no feelings. None whatsoever. One of the girls came and covered me up. Richard walked up to me and removed the shawl. Something snapped and I simply unhooked my bra and sat there. I got up when I needed to use the restroom and walked through the club half naked as Richard's eyes followed me. I didn't care anymore.

Richard raged at me all through the night, throwing me against the wall, bashing my head against the tub, and raping me several times. But I didn't cry or say a word, which made him more brutal. By morning, I could hardly walk, so Richard had them bring a wheelchair to the room. The young lady helped me into the car, and I thanked her.

When we got to the house, I crawled to the bed, pulled the sheets over my head, and stayed there. It was Dante's inferno and the flames of Hades had consumed me. Richard was oblivious to my situation. He got up the next morning and went to work and didn't return for another two days. When he got home, he changed and left again. I was in that bed for a whole week. I didn't eat, brush my teeth, or comb my hair. Tears wet my pillow and something in my heart died. I wondered why my parents had not called. Later I would find out that Richard had called to tell them that

I had the flu, which had turned into pneumonia, and they should keep Caleb until I was better.

I stayed in the dark. The only good news was that Richard made sure I had juice. He would leave a bottle of orange juice by my bed and that was what I drank during my time in bed. I began to hallucinate. I would see elephants flying, the room would turn upside down. I was losing my mind. But I sank deeper into my bed and at some point, I couldn't get up to use the bathroom, so I started urinating in the bed and Richard started using a face mask in the room. He would prop me up and give me the orange juice. I melted into the darkness.

Chapter *16*

From somewhere in the distance I could hear Momma and Pop's voices.

"Allie Pooh!" And the voices were getting closer.

Then I closed my eyes and found myself falling into a bottomless abyss. I saw Pop's face and Momma was holding her arms out to me. All my neighbors at Sunset Street were there, including Ms. Washington, but I slipped through them without touching them, floating through a cloud of cotton. I would never go home again. Then something began to happen. I saw a giant hand break my fall. I fell into that hand and instantly I was moving in the opposite direction.

I opened my eyes and saw Momma and Pop staring at me. I also noticed Ms. Washington standing by my bed.

"Where am I?"

"Cedars-Sinai hospital."

"Why?"

"You've been very sick, Allie Pooh," Pop whispered.

Then I remembered, "Oh gosh! Where is my son?" I became agitated.

"He is safe. He's with Adey."

"Adey?"

"Yes. He is watching him while we all watch you."

"This is all confusing. Where is Richard?"

"In jail, where he belongs!" Pop retorted.

"Well, he's been released to his parents," Momma explained.

"Because he was poisoning you! That's why!"

"Poison! How?"

"Remember the orange juice he gave you? Well, it seems there was codeine and acetaminophen in the juice. These are dangerous, slow poisons in these excessive amounts. He says he was simply medicating you for your pain."

"But why would he want to kill you, Allie?"

I stared into space. I didn't know where to begin.

"Richard is a troubled man, Momma."

"Not troubled. He is evil," she hissed. "He tried to kill you, Allie! He tried to kill you!"

"Let us focus on Allie!" Pop declared. He held my hands and said, "I knew you would come back to me. We refused to let you go, child. Evil cannot drive a trailer through the Smiths' paradise. The mistake we made was to allow it to park in our garage."

"God is good," I heard Ms. Washington declare.

Someone came through the door and I noticed that it was one of the pastors from the church.

"Hello, Pastor Jenkins. She's alive!" Momma said.

"Praise his name!" the pastor said.

Pastor Jenkins stayed for a while. As he was getting ready to leave, he stood up, held my hands, and said, "Bishop Blake and Mother Mae send their prayers and love. They will be happy when I report to them that you are back with us in this land of the living. The whole church is praying for you."

"Thank you, Pastor Jenkins."

He said a prayer and with that, he left. Right after that came a stream of people from Sunset Street. I fell in and out of sleep as they made their way to my room. When I finally woke up, Ebony and Shade were the only ones in my room sitting by my bed.

"She's back!" Shade exclaimed when I opened my eyes.

Ebony started wailing. The type of hot tears that erupt like lava and before long a mesmerizing force had invaded the room as the three of us were wailing. I for the grief and pain of the last seven years and my girls for my grief that they saw, though they didn't know the half of it.

"I will personally kill that bastard!" Shade yelled.

Ebony and I looked at Shade, the quiet one, and busted out laughing. It was so funny that that statement would come out of Shade's mouth.

"Stop laughing! I am serious. I will kill him with my bare hands."

"Shade, you can't kill an ant."

And we giggled some more until all three of us started laughing uncontrollably. The nurses came in to see what was happening in my room, first the wailing and now laughter. We held hands and fell into silence. Words were insufficient.

Chapter 17

I met with Richard in a dream so vivid that I thought it was happening in real life.

"Hello, Alero."

At some point in the marriage, Richard had decided Allie was not regal and mature enough. He called me Alero. I responded because it was my name.

"Hello, Richard."

"Please sit."

"No, I prefer to stand," I said. "I am here because I want to tell you that I will not be taking you to court."

"Thank you!"

"Not yet anyway," I clarified. "Don't thank me. I am not doing it for you. It's for Caleb. And here is what I want in return. Did you bring the prenuptial agreement?"

"Yes."

"Read it!"

"What do you mean?"

"Read it out loud!"

Richard read it and it was exactly what I thought it would be except for the part that said if the marriage didn't last a year, I had to pay back all the money spent on the wedding and return the ring.

"I knew something shady was hiding in that prenuptial you all made me sign. Do you know that this won't even hold up a court of law? Is that the original copy?"

"Yes."

"Okay, give it to me."

I put it in my purse. "Richard, you are damaged goods, an evil soul. Your nanny came to see me a few weeks ago."

"Elizabeth came to see you!" He acted surprised.

"Yes, she did."

Richard shook his head in shame.

"She reiterated the story you told me about the heinous acts in the Braithwaite home and a bit more than you shared with me. She saw everything. As she walked into my hospital room, I knew she was on a mission. She is ready to testify against all of you whenever I ask. She believes your mother is a slave, but the men are evil except for you. She said you were tormented as a child and as such didn't have a choice. I disagree, though. At some point, we all start making our own choices. You almost destroyed me but all the love and care from Pop and Momma and Ms. Washington and Adey and Ebony and Shade were building blocks. My roots are deep in love, Richard, and you couldn't destroy me. You tried and failed. So here is the deal I've worked out with the district attorney's office. You will be on probation for twenty years—"

"Twenty years!" he cried out.

I held out my hand for him to stop and said, "Or you can go to prison for the rest of your life. There is no way a judge and jury wouldn't convict you." He fell silent.

"You will attend therapy for the rest of those twenty years and send attendance logs to the DA's office each month."

"I can do that!" He sounded happy.

"I have a list of four therapists here, you must choose one of them."

I handed him a list.

"So, I can't choose mine?"

"No, you can't. Next, you will not contact Caleb until he's twenty-five years old. Then you can explain to him what a disaster I saved him from. Your parents are not to contact me, my family, or Caleb or be near him. You will relinquish your parental rights. You will have them fax you their agreement to relinquish any of their rights to him in writing before I leave this office. You will transfer his share of the inheritance into the account in this document. All must be done before I leave this office. Everything I said is stipulated in this document. You may sign after you've transferred my son's inheritance into his account."

"I need my attorney to review this."

"No, you don't! Remember I had no attorney with me when you all made me sign a prenup in the middle of the night. If I leave this office without those papers, I am walking straight to the district attorney's office and we will be taking you to court, Richard."

"Okay, there is no need to threaten!"

"This is not a threat! It is a promise."

"I need to call my father. I will need a few hours."

"Richard, you have thirty minutes. I will wait right here!"

Richard went into a private room and within twenty minutes was out. He handed me three pages: one was a letter from his parents relinquishing any rights over Caleb, the second was Richard's letter relinquishing his rights, and the third was the bank transfer.

"These two documents are unacceptable. It needs to be witnessed by an attorney or notarized. You have ten minutes."

"That's been unrealistic," he complained.

"Richard! Don't tell me what seems unrealistic! You have ten minutes, or I am walking out of this office."

He went into the conference room. I saw his minions scrambling to meet the deadline. One of the attorneys walked into the room and tried to talk sense but the voice of the older Braithwaite on the phone was loud and clear, "Give her whatever she wants!" Richard walked back to his office with a minute to spare.

"Here you are, Alero." He was melancholic.

I was satisfied with the documents and put them in my briefcase. "You may sign now."

He took a pen and signed the papers.

"So how much of the money are you getting?" he asked.

"I do not want a penny of your money. However, your son deserves all that he will get. I hope he can donate some of the money to abused children in this country. My God will have mercy on you."

"How can you still talk of God after all you've been through?"

"How can I not talk to the one who saved me from a monster? Go to church, Richard. Allow the messages in the church to penetrate your heart. Maybe you can find salvation."

"Maybe I will. Thank you."

"You thought you took the best of me but the thing about a soul is that you can't take what was never yours. You never had me, so I was never yours to take. You abused the parts of me that were accessible to you and all I can ask is that God forgives you. I am giving you an opportunity to save your soul because if you don't, you will eventually get what you deserve. My sincere hope is that you all find healing, restoration, something! Because you are a sick bunch. Hell can't be worse than your lives."

"I apologize." Richard moved towards me.

"Please keep your apologies! Goodbye!"

Chapter *18*

I was home on Sunset Street. The comfort of the blue drapes and the slightly crooked bend of the coffee table that Pop had made when I was a teenager. Momma and Pop had taken Caleb with them to run errands. I was still in a daze. I couldn't believe that I had gone through all that. I was an abused woman, married to a monster who'd tried to kill me, and now I'd opened my eyes to the love of my life. He was comforting me but I didn't think he knew that he was the reason I hadn't died in that bed. Adey had kept appearing to me in my daze, telling me to hold on and that I could not die. What had taken him so long and why was he here? I was starting to feel anger well up within me when I heard Adey say, "Let me make you something to eat, Allie." The anger immediately got buried as I responded to Adey. It had always been this way. I would think that I should be angry at him but then, he reeled me back in. I should have been giving him a piece of my mind but here we were in the kitchen making pancakes or at least pretending to make pancakes. Because Adey had decided he was a teenager again and sprinkled some flour on me and immediately we were laughing and running around the kitchen throwing flour at each other.

"Your mom will have a fit if she walks in on us."

"You better clean it up before she gets here, then," I responded.

"Well let me get to it," Adey said.

"I'm thirsty," I yawned.

"Let me get you something."

"No worries, I'll get it. Thank you."

I opened the refrigerator and the only thing I saw was the gallon of orange juice staring at me. It kept growing bigger and bigger until I felt it would swallow me whole. I took the gallon of orange juice and began to smash it against the sink. Screaming and yelling at the orange juice as it spilled all over the floor. Adey watched from afar and I was grateful he didn't come closer because I might have smashed the jug on his head. I was mad. Mad at allowing myself to be that woman. I kept screaming, "How did I get here? How? How? How? How did he turn me into this person?" I was furious at the world. At Richard and his family. Eventually I was spent and stopped smashing the box and looked at Adey.

"I'm sorry."

"Never apologize," he said, moving close to me. "You will get better. I promise."

"You don't know that," I replied.

Then I had a flashback to the ring Adey had given me when we were children. I got up as if in a trance and walked towards my bedroom. I opened the mirrored jewelry box brightly painted with beautiful flowers that Momma had gotten me for my sixteenth birthday. I opened it and there the ring was, resting on the tiny pillow insert. I pulled the ring out. It looked so innocent so real and I felt tainted. I flung the ring against the wall. I was dirty. Polluted! I ran into the bathroom still fully clothed and turned on the shower. I could feel waves crashing again as the water hit my body. I let out a scream and kept screaming. I don't know how long I was there until Adey walked in and carried me out to the living room sofa. We sat in silence in the pool of water that had gathered around me. Adey's stillness quieted my raising heartbeat. He started drying my hair but I stopped him and asked him to step out. Adey found the ring, picked it up, and gently kissed it. I smiled as he placed our beginning into the box. He closed the jewelry box. I closed my eyes and exhaled.

The door opened and we watched Momma and Caleb and Pop take in the scene as they walked into the kitchen. Adey tried to explain but Momma held up a finger, her way of saying that no explanation was needed. "Caleb, help me clean up here. Pop, bring your daughter to the living room."

I allowed Pop and Adey to walk me out of there, but not before I had given Caleb a bear hug. We both needed it. I could see that he needed an explanation but I couldn't do it today. I went to my room, took some melatonin, and drifted off.

I woke up with Adey and Caleb sitting by the bed talking.

"Why are you still here, Adey?"

"Uncle Adey was telling me all the adventures you all had when you were younger."

"Oh no!" I groaned. "Did he tell you about the fire that sent us to Beverly Hills for the weekend?"

"Yes, how did you know?" he queried.

"I'm a mind reader," I joked.

"And, Mommy, I've decided that I will also become a neurosurgeon."

"Really! You've decided, huh?"

"Yes, Mommy! I have made that decision and uncle will be my mentor."

I looked at Adey, who smiled.

I shook my head and teased, "I see you haven't lost your touch."

"I'm an innocent bystander. I am glad that you slept, though."

"Yes, me too," Caleb said.

"Caleb, would you go finish your homework now? We can talk about cadavers before I leave."

"Sure!" And he dashed to his room.

"What are you doing to my kid?"

"Nothing! You've done a great job, Allie! You should be proud of Caleb!"

"I should be worried."

"No, he has a good head on his shoulders. However, that leads me to what I want to discuss with you."

"I'm all ears."

"I know that you are a psychologist, however, sometimes it's difficult for those of us in the helping profession to get help ourselves. I believe you have post-traumatic stress disorder."

"I think so too."

"Maybe you should see someone?"

"Maybe I should but there is something I must do first."

"What is that?"

"Learn to shoot."

"What?"

"Don't be so surprised."

"I am not! I mean, I can understand. And I can teach you."

"Really? When did you learn?"

"Long story but I had a friend who was from the South and hunting was their pastime. I had to learn to shoot."

"Thanks, but no, I will find a teacher at the shooting range."

"I will come with you, then."

"No, Adey. I have to do this alone."

"Okay, but can you take up the shooting and still find a therapist?"

"Well, that could work." The thought of holding the metal of a gun suddenly gave me strength. I got up from the bed and said, "I will schedule two appointments tomorrow. One to see a therapist and the other to learn to kill."

Adey's jaw dropped but I walked out of the bedroom.

Chapter 19

The thing about trauma is that it hijacks your body. How could I dislodge this parasite that was eating me alive? My therapist, Dr. Carry, explained that just like animals shook off their traumas, humans must learn to also do the trauma shake by becoming active. So I purchased running gear from the athletic store in Upland. My first attempt was excruciating. I thought my lungs would explode as I tried to complete a one-mile run at the high school track. But I was determined to complete this shake so I intended to be back again and again.

The therapy sessions were helpful. I had been told not to try to understand what had happened to me because the cognitive part of my brain had been hijacked during the fighter-flight response. I also learned that my silence during the ordeal had been a defense mechanism. I would have been killed if I had tried to fight or flee so I froze. I was stronger than I thought. But I was still angry. Angry at all the Braithwaites and I wanted them to be scared for their life.

My shooting lessons were progressing well and I got to pick out a gun. I had refused Adey's involvement. This was something that I needed to do myself. Actually, I was avoiding him altogether. I was angry at him too but did not have the emotional space to deal with him at the moment. I made my way to the gun shop on Crenshaw and the salesperson, Jose, a burly Latino man, gave me a good tutorial. He recommended beginners get the 9 mm. He wanted to know if it was for home protection and I said it was to protect myself. "In that case, we recommend that you don't look for a gun with an external safety."

"Wait! What? You want to sell me an unsafe gun?" It was at that moment I chided myself for coming to Crenshaw for this important equipment. Now I had this Jose trying to sell me an unsafe gun. As I tried to figure out a way of exiting the story, Jose responded, "The mind is the best safety. In the heat of the moment during a self-defense situation, you might forget to disengage the safety."

It was then I remembered that my gun trainer had told me the same thing. She said, "Allie, you must remember to store your gun properly but don't use an external safety because you might forget."

"I see!" I responded to Jose.

Jose also lectured me about getting a night sight since most assaults occurred at night. I wondered why Richard had never learned that lesson. I'd been assaulted pretty much anytime of the day. He was an indiscriminate abuser. Night and day meant nothing to the Braithwaites. Finally, Jose recommended five handguns and we decided the Glock 19 was the best selection. Jose swore that would be the one gun he'd want on him in any situation. I decided on the Gen 3 model because it was great for range, nightstand, and concealing.

I paid for the gun.

Chapter 20

I also got Caleb into therapy. I couldn't shield him from the mess. I watched as Caleb and his new best friend, George, played video games in the family room. On the surface, he seemed well adjusted. He was top of his class, respectful, and none of this mess seemed to have ruffled him, but I knew better. Adverse childhood experiences can be debilitating and become complex. It is like when your earring gets caught in a web of necklaces and you can't seem to find the thread that unknots the web. The more you try to tease out the earring, the more it gets jumbled. I also feared there might be a genetic proclivity. Was the son of a pervert also a pervert? The knot in my head fell into my stomach until my entire body was swallowed in pain. I remembered seeing him for the first time, my beautiful angel nursing at my breast at six pounds, ten ounces. Lauryn Hill's song "To Zion" was on auto play in my head—"I've never been in love like this before." It was the rising of a California sunshine after a foggy morning. It radiated through my veins and pumped joy into my being. My heart was bursting within me as I smiled at the bundle of joy and he healed me. Instantly, without permission, he pulled me together again. Richard had been uncomfortable and left the room as soon as he could but nothing dimmed my joy. That little being hadn't asked to be born and I had been determined to wrap him in enough love to erase the indignities of his bloodline.

Trauma is personal. You must walk this journey one step at a time. We were discussing protective factors in therapy. Dr. Carry said that they inoculated us from victimhood. Protective factors included a good supportive family environment. I wasn't sure that I provided that for Caleb. With Richard gone all the time, I had him to myself, but he also had my parents and Ms. Washington and all my friends. Were those enough? Would my child turn out okay?

"A penny for your thoughts?" Pop interrupted.

I turned to look at him with tears streaming down my face.

"Allie Pooh! My daughter!" He pulled me to himself and I held on for dear life.

"Pop, may I ask you something?"

"Anything, my girl!"

"Will Caleb ever be whole? Does he have evil in him like his dad?" I cried.

"Look at me, child." He propped me up so I could look at him.

"First, is his therapist concerned for him?"

"No, his therapist actually says he's riding the storm quite well. He knows that the divorce is not his fault, but I am still concerned."

"You become like those who raise you not those who birth you. We all together will provide the safe space my grandson needs to thrive. Now listen to me. He will have his struggles in life like we all do but if we give him the right life nutrition, the odds will work in his favor. You can do your part and leave the rest to the Almighty. Let him make up the differences.

"You might walk with a limp for now, Allie Pooh, but you will be stronger moving forward. You will make a difference. Your story will make a difference. When you are ready, start telling it.

"And one more thing. You are grieving and don't see clearly yet, but stop keeping him from Adey. That man will make a good son out of that boy. Leave them alone."

I nodded in agreement. None of it made sense yet but I nodded to end the conversation. I walked over to Caleb and hugged him.

"Mommy, are you okay?"

"Of course, I am. How about I play a game with you two? Two against one."

"Yes, Mommy! Bring it on."

I knew what I needed to do. It was time.

The next day, I got in my car around ten in the morning and got on the freeway towards Napa. I couldn't tell you how long it took, but I drove with focus and attention to every detail of the murders I was planning. I knew I could get in because all the security and staff loved me as much as they disliked or hated their employers. I arrived at the prison that the monsters called home and everything went according to plan. My phone had been ringing off the hook. First, it was Momma, then Pop called, and, of course, Adey called too. All I could think of when I saw his name flash on the screen was where had he been all those years—he'd abandoned me.

This battle I had to win for Caleb. They all had to die. I would go to prison but at least Caleb would be rid of the Braithwaite demons. I was escorted to the living room and right in front of me were all three of them, Richard and his mom and dad. I smiled at them. It could not have been better.

"Welcome, Alero!" Claire said. "We are so excited that you've come to us. We can talk and get all this behind us."

She ushered me in. I took everything in and allowed her to point me to a chair. Richard followed like a lost puppy while his father pushed him towards me. He sat next to me and the next thing I knew, Richard was on the floor, kicking and screaming, asking for forgiveness. We all watched him. His dad kept yelling, "Shut up, Richard!" But the screams got louder and I was getting annoyed at this man. This was my day and I would not allow him to ruin it for me. I got up and slapped him as hard as I could. "Shut up, Richard!"

He ran out of the room and we all watched as he ran up the stairs. Claire began to apologize for her son and her husband reached for his phone to probably call on one of his cronies to bail him out of this situation. The Braithwaites were not used to a public display of emotions and Richard had disoriented them.

"I will not shut up, Dad!" We all heard Richard scream as he rushed back to the room. I looked his way and, to my dismay, Richard was waving a gun in the air.

"Shit!" I cried. "Richard what are you doing?"

"Shut up, Alero, and sit down."

Oh no, he didn't, I thought.

"Not today, you idiot! You will never again tell me what to do, you moron," I screamed at him.

I pounced at him. But he brushed me aside and walked towards his parents, who were staring at him.

"Dad, you are a monster and you turned me into one. I hate you and despise everything about you. I hate myself. Do you understand me? I hate myself."

"Lower your voice, Richard. The household staff can hear you. And put that gun down."

"I don't care who hears because you do not have a hold on me anymore. And I will not put the gun down." He pointed the gun at his dad and pulled the trigger.

It was all happening in slow motion. Richard turned to his mother and all I could hear over the screams of the household staff was, "I hate you too. You are a piece-of-trash mother and you will never control me again. You two belong in hell." Richard shot and killed his mother.

I sat there seething with anger. *This fool! You will not deny me my revenge. I will kill you myself.* I took out my gun and aimed at him but was grabbed by the chef, who dragged me to the kitchen.

"Look here, Mrs. Braithwaite," he began.

"Do not call me that! Call me Allie."

"Allie, put the gun in your purse and drink this cup of water. These people are not worth you going to jail for. Do not become like them. Let them kill themselves and this world will be rid of their evil. Please wait here a few minutes before coming out. Think of Caleb." At the mention of my son, my mind seemed to switch back into alignment. I couldn't believe I had contemplated murder and actually wanted to kill. I dropped the gun and ran out of the kitchen. I watched as the cops escorted Richard off the property in handcuffs. He had killed his parents and he was smiling as he walked out the door.

I went back to the kitchen to thank the chef. I picked up the gun and drove back to Crenshaw. Jose recognized me. I reached into my purse, took out the gun, laid it on the counter, and walked back to my car.

I drove home to Caleb.

Chapter 21

Caleb and I had moved to Claremont, a city located approximately thirty miles east of Los Angeles. I needed to be swaddled in the warmth of this village, with its hundreds of acres of developed parks and tree-lined streets. I enjoy walking with Caleb through the acclaimed Claremont Colleges, a consortium of five undergraduate and two graduate higher education institutions. The community took pride in its safety and rich cultural, educational, and architectural heritage. The village coffee shop and vegetarian café where the cheeky teenagers and shop owners got out of their way to say, "Hey, Allie," or, "Hello, Dr. A," or my favorite, "How was Caleb's science competition last night?" Always something specific to make me feel at home. A place where my name was known. Like my Sunset Street experience. I taught psychology as a part-time faculty at the Claremont McKenna College, which also meant that I got stopped and waved at by students as they rushed past me going to class or catching up with their own lives. I loved people watching, the creative types dressed to stand out, the stay-at-home mothers pushing their strollers and toddlers in concert, middle-aged men jogging, or college students rushing to the next thing on their daily agenda. The feel of Claremont was not the familial intimacy of Sunset Street; this was a different type of bonding—academic, creative, a cohesiveness of lifestyle.

I was a working woman. In addition to teaching, I'd moved my family law practice to Indian Hills, along the foothills in Claremont, and developed a large-scale pro bono practice for abused women. I'd added two partners, so the law firm was known as Smith, Logan, and Bakare. Teresa Logan was a white woman who was a law school friend. She was one of the toughest attorneys I knew but with a heart of gold. She'd grown up in the hood. The Logans were still one of the few white families left in the neighborhood. She knew that she wasn't Black but the sista could flow. Teresa was a defense attorney specializing in criminal law. Beatrice Bakare, B2 as we called her, was a Nigerian American attorney who specialized in international litigation, including immigration. We were seeing more of these types of cases. B2 was a force of nature. She would surely go on to argue before the Supreme Court or at least become a judge, she was that good. I was glad she'd decided to set up shop for the time being with Smith, Logan, and Bakare. We also had ten other first- and second-year attorneys working for us.

My parents had rented out the house on Sunset Street and found a house across the street from Caleb and me. Caleb had two homes. He could walk across the street to either of them. If I needed milk, all Caleb had to do was walk over to grab some from Pop and Momma's kitchen. Momma shopped for an army, so I never needed to do much grocery shopping, and whatever we needed was available in her pantry.

Adey worked at Loma Linda hospital as a neurosurgeon but still got calls from Cedars and across the nation to take on a second chair or to give an opinion. Each minute we had together was sacred. We'd gotten into the habit of trying all the family-owned restaurants in our area for our weekend lunches as opposed to the chains in our bid of keeping the currency local.

"Is your mom home? I don't feel like going out today," I said to Adey.

"We can go to my place whether Mom is home or not. But she isn't home, to respond to your original question."

"Okay. Once she hears the car, you know she's coming out to say hello, which usually takes about an hour," I joked. We both laughed. Ms. Washington lived with Adey when she was in the city. She'd become busier now than when we were younger. She had merged speaking and singing. A full-fledged motivational speaker on *Ask Ms. Washington Live!* a radio talk show that commanded a national audience. She was presently in the UK on a tour for her new book, *Authentically Me!*

Adey lived in San Antonio Heights, otherwise known as the Beverly Hills of the Inland Empire. It was an exclusive area and he'd bought the most beautiful home in the hills of Upland, which came with a guesthouse, where Ms. Washington lived. The guesthouse was bigger than my entire house, with three large bedrooms, a den, and two bathrooms. The main house was a sprawling mansion with four bedrooms and about seven bathrooms. There were four or five gardens on the property, hiking trails that went down to the Claremont Colleges.

We drove to Adey's house. The drive there felt like stepping into a retreat, Adey's bit of paradise.

"Do you want something to eat? Let's get some food and talk out here."

I'd fallen in love with the property before stepping inside the first time Adey and I came with his realtor to view this place. There were indoor and outdoor sitting areas surrounded by a lavender garden, labyrinth path for meditation, and a micro-organic farm fed by spring water. A lily pond and a gazebo were frequented by deer and beautiful butterflies in the summer. The property had an amazing view of the mountains and beautiful sunrises and sunsets and was the best place I knew for stargazing.

Cecilia, Adey's housekeeper and chef, was always excited to see me.

"Como estas, Cecilia!" I noticed her reading in the garden.

"Estoy muy bien, Ms. Allie!"

I smiled. My Spanish is limited.

"What would you like me to get for you?" she asked.

"Nothing, please continue reading. Adey and I will grab something to eat."

Cecilia was an excellent cook and housekeeper. I was sure that there would be more than enough food in the refrigerator. She made sure her boss was fully stocked. Adey and I went to the kitchen and found some Thai shrimp salad, grabbed some wine and crackers from the pantry. Adey added some steak and rice and black beans to his plate.

"Grab some condiments," he stated.

"Yes, sir," I teased.

"Please and thank you, my darling."

"Much better."

"And some water too."

"Anything else?" I asked.

I placed all the items in a basket, which Adey carried to our favorite place in the lavender garden. We ate in silence and Adey poured some wine.

This place was a beautiful piece of earth. I could hear the birds chirping and squirrels scurrying.. I needed a clear head to say what I needed to say.

"I'm all ears," Adey said.

Adey knew when I wanted to talk without me having to say anything. He doted on me like a pop bear.

"It's been over two years since you came back, and you haven't told me why you cut me off. I need to know why."

He took a breath. "When I got to Harvard, the loneliness drove me insane. I knew I would miss you, but I wasn't ready for the wrenching that happened. It was as if my oxygen had been cut off and I had to find a way to breathe again. It felt like my right arm had been amputated and I had to learn to use my left arm, which proved to be tremendously difficult. Life was at a standstill. I was a ship without a compass. I wrote you letters the first two years, which I never sent, but it never got better, Allie Pooh! I was dying without you, but I didn't want it to be your problem. After a while, I felt too despondent to write and almost went into full-blown depression. A few years later, I got on the plane and flew to LAX. I simply needed to see you, but I got to your apartment and saw you with some guy. Now I know the guy was Richard."

"Are you serious?"

"I was angry at myself and thought, 'What did you fly all the way here for? If you love her so much, let her live her life.' I turned right around and boarded a flight back to Boston."

"Oh, my goodness! You came here and didn't see me. You are incredulous, Adey, but do you know that happened to me too?" I proceeded to tell him about my trip to Boston.

"Seeing you and that girl paralyzed me and I had the same thoughts you did. What happened next for you?"

"I returned to Harvard a different person. There was no reason to pine after you. I had met Cheyenne my first year on campus and she introduced me to life on campus. She was Native American and interested in genealogy and family history. She encouraged me to find my father. I reached out to him. I know where he lives in Lagos. Cheyenne was also deeply spiritual and encouraged me to find my center, so I chose spirituality. I started creating peace and praying more. Cheyenne was my saving grace. I wasn't missing you as much and was determined to make something of myself. I was so involved in my studies and getting fellowships that I lost sight of the world outside."

"What happened with Cheyenne?" I asked.

"I proposed to her. Cheyenne wasn't you but I could live with our stability. She was happy and we were supposed to visit her parents that weekend to share the news. I walked her to the parking structure and she got into her yellow Saab. I teased that she was a cop magnet. You could spot her sunflower-yellow car from miles away. We kissed good night."

I waited for Adey to continue and when he didn't, I looked up to see tears rolling down his face.

"Adey, it's okay. I understand that you had a life on the East Coast."

"I never saw her again, Allie."

"What do you mean?"

"Cheyenne was involved in a multivehicle accident and her car spun till she faced oncoming traffic. She was hit by an oncoming car. She died on the way to the hospital."

"Oh, Adey!" I held his hands and wept with him. I cried for his broken heart. I wept for Cheyenne.

"I am grateful for her," I said.

"Why?" Adey asked.

"She took my place."

"No one can take your place."

"I know how you get, Adey. She didn't allow you to crawl into a dark hole."

"Yeah!" he agreed.

"I'm sorry, Adey."

"I'm sorry too. I kept thinking maybe she knew deep down that I didn't want to marry her. Maybe that's why she was distracted."

"Or maybe she was happy, Adey! Maybe she died with a knowing that she was loved."

"I hope so!"

"Look at me. I married the first person who proposed to me and then got mad at you because you weren't here to stop it."

"I came to your wedding to see for myself. It was officially the most devastating moment of my life. Well, that was until I had to watch you almost die in the hospital."

I told Adey everything about my marriage and all the details I'd spared him the first time I told this story. I shared about being left on the street of Vegas and being stuffed in the back of the car another time. I told him that I knew I was being poisoned and welcomed it because I wanted to die. I confessed how ashamed I was that I'd arrived at this place. This wasn't supposed to happen to me. It was like I'd felt abandoned by Adey when I didn't hear from him, so I'd jumped into this relationship. I didn't spare him any details. My therapist thought I was ready to share this with him and not be retraumatized. I was surprised at the ease at which the words rolled off my lips. By the time I finished, Adey was pacing the garden—furious!

"Why have you kept this?"

"I have to think of Caleb!"

"You have to think of yourself. Allie Pooh, do you mind if I take a walk? I will be back honestly, but I really need to clear my head."

"I understand!" I said.

I knew this would be difficult for anyone who loved me, but I felt Adey needed to know. I also knew that he could handle this better than Momma and Pop because Adey has had intense trauma therapy. He was in a good place.

I watched Adey put on his running shoes to hike the trail. I knew he would be back. Our kind of love was deep enough for both of us to sink into, get lost and found, and still float to the surface for air. I laid in the hammock overlooking the citrus orchard and fell asleep.

Butterfly kisses across my face. I opened my eyes and saw Adey smiling. I smiled back. All was well in the world. We had floated to the top. He climbed into the hammock and straddled me so I was looking up at him and he stared with tears forming.

"Allie Pooh, I've loved you from the moment I laid my eyes on you. When your dad asked me to take care of you, I took it to heart and I did it with all my heart at that young age. I am sorry I left you. I am sorry you went through all that mess. My heart is broken for the misery you went through alone. The pain of all you went through cuts through me like razors. I wasn't there to save you. I don't ever want to be away from you ever again. Nothing matters this much to me. I want to protect you. I want to be the one you wake up next to. I want to love you every moment of the day. I want to make up for the lost time. I want to heal you. I'm so sorry. I've always been yours. I was never good for any other woman."

I sat up and held him tight and he held on to me for dear life as rocked gently in the hammock.

"I love you Alero 'Allie Pooh' Smith! I want to spend the rest of my life with you."

At that moment, I saw it as clear as day. He was the one I'd been waiting for and he'd been there all the time. I heard sounds and trumpets, whistles and bells, angels descending and ascending.

"My darling Adey. I can't contain this moment. It's as if yesterday never happened. I'm here with you. I'm home and I'm yours."

"Allie Pooh, I've wasted so many years and all roads lead to you. I will ask you to marry me properly soon, but what say you?"

"You'll find out when you ask me," I teased.

Chapter 22

I was having lunch with Shade and Ebony at Adey's house, our new Sunset Street. I had the key so I'd become a partial resident because Adey was hardly home and he wanted Caleb and I to make use of it. "Allie, please bring Caleb here, have parties . . . Have Pop barbecue here on Sundays. I bought this place for all of us. I know it can't replace Sunset Street, but it's close," Adey explained.

"Well, let's call it Sunset Street," I joked.   The next time I visited, I was met with a sign that read Sunset Street.

Ms. Washington, Pop and Momma, and my girlfriends all loved the idea. Ever since, Adey's house had become the place to be. I'd invited my girls over to tell them about the murder I'd almost attempted. They sat shell-shocked.

"Girl, this is crazy, you could be in jail," Ebony yelled.

"Shhh," Shade tried to shush Ebony. "Allie, this is crazy! You mean you went there by yourself?"

"I can't explain it! It felt like an out-of-body experience. I really wanted to wipe out all traces of the Braithwaites so Caleb wouldn't have to deal with them."

Shade stood up and pulled me into an embrace. Ebony joined and all of us hugged.

"Are you seeing a therapist?" Ebony asked.

"You know I am," I responded.

"Well, this is the type of shit you should be sharing with the therapist because, girl, the truth is I would have gone to the house with you to kill someone. That man makes my blood boil when I remember what he did to you."

"You should have called us, seriously," Shade joined. "Please don't put yourself in that kind of situation again. We are sisters for life and we got your back."

"Well, there won't be a next time because they are either dead or in prison."

"We have to watch that mess because I don't want him getting out on parole," Shade ventured.

"Such a coward! Why didn't he take his own life too?" Ebony asked.

"I don't know but it doesn't matter because he was given life without parole."

"Throw away the keys! Good riddance!" Ebony retorted. "Mehn, I need counseling just listening to this mess."

"You are right! I will give you my therapist's phone number. Y'all need counseling anyway," I teased.

"Okay, let's move this party to my favorite place in this house," Ebony said.

We moved to Adey's gazebo, which was nestled in a sprawling garden.

"Here is the oasis!" Ebony purred.

It was the cushy bed, large enough for at least three lounging ladies, that was the main attraction. We each selected a pillow and stretched on the bed. I watched my girls and shed a tear.

Shade said, "Allie, please don't cry."

"Girl, let the sista cry. She's been through the wringer," Ebony reasoned.

"These are tears of joy," I said. "This was what Richard wanted to keep me from. All of you!"

"And he failed big time!" the others responded.

"Let's get some wine," Ebony said.

Celia, as if on cue, brought some vintage wine.

No one could have asked for a better friendship as it spanned a teary past, down to memories to be told our unborn children. We sat down under the ambience of mildly swaying winds with our feet up.

Ebony, wanting to change the subject, asked, "Shade, so tell us, the most amazing part of your trip to Egypt, I know you won't leave a sista guessing, right?"

Shade chuckled, crossed her legs, and started recounting memorable moments from her Egyptian tour.

"Ebony, do you know the funny things about Egypt that amazed me?" she asked with a full grin. And before Ebony could pick up her response lines, Shades had started.

Shade continued her detailed description of the pyramids. My eyes met Ebony's and we knew what to do.

"Hmm, ladies, we all need to make this trip together to save Shades this lengthy explanation. Meanwhile, I say we toast to the pyramids!" Ebony said. We all laughed out loud, including Shade, as this was a trick we'd started in childhood to keep Shade from boring us with details.

I held my wine glass and clinked it against Ebony's before Shade could continue with her narrative.

Chapter *23*

They say love is like a drug, once you taste it, you keep searching wells to find more. I inhaled Adey's scent as I laid wrapped in his arms, I felt completely known. A worship! A complete surrender of wills. I laid in his arms, swallowed up in waves and waves of sweet dust of joy that crawled from the tiny curl of my toes and made their way up slowly into pathways of cells and corridors of joy.

This was what it was supposed to feel like. I had always assumed Adey had stayed a virgin, like me, through high school. It was something we didn't really talk about. Even if he was a virgin when we were teenagers, I was certain at some point in college he must have had sex with a girlfriend. Adey wasn't the type of man to have flings.

I hadn't had much experience with sex; very early on in my life, I'd decided I was going to save myself for my husband. In college, while other girls were partying and experimenting, my roommate, Jennifer, and I kept to ourselves.

Jennifer was a shy girl, a Christian that sang for her fellowship on campus. I was shocked when I found a raunchy novel under her pillow. As I read, the words jumped off the page, creating powerful images in my mind.

The dampness was new to me. With every touch and every kiss the dashing male gave his beloved, my body shivered. I found myself unable to put down the book. I remember the first time Ebony had sex with

Marshawn, all she could talk about for weeks was how in love she was. I was more concerned about her getting pregnant.

On our first night together, Adey wanted to hold back, but I was ready. Hell, I'd waited my whole life for this.

We started with dinner at a lovely restaurant Adey had picked out. I was strangely anxious at the beginning of the date, but after a few glasses of wine, I relaxed and was laughing at Adey's stories from medical school. After dinner, he took me home. We sat in the car for some minutes, talking. More like he listened, while I talked. I told him the story of how Shade, Ebony, and I had gotten kicked out of a basketball game. One of the players had tackled Marshawn; in a split second, Ebony was on the court, ready to fight. Shade and I jumped in to restrain her. I choked with laughter as I ended the story, "They dragged us right off the court."

Adey smiled and looked at me. He had a look I had never seen before. "You are so beautiful."

I smiled and looked away. He continued, "It's crazy you have no idea how sexy you are."

I never thought being referred to as sexy could be so empowering.

"Can I kiss you?"

I smiled and nodded. It was all I could do; my tongue had dried up in my mouth. Adey leaned in and kissed me gently on the lips. He paused and looked deep into my eyes. His breath hit my face. I stared back into his eyes. We were lost.

He leaned in and kissed me again, longer and harder this time. He broke off the kiss. "I'm sure Caleb is waiting for you. I should go home."

There was no way I was letting him leave after that. "Caleb is at my parents'."

Adey took the cue. In less than five minutes we were in my bedroom. He stared at me like I was a supermodel. He pulled me into his arms and whispered, "We can wait, my love." I didn't want to.

Life was perfect. Adey and I spent our days filled with work and family and nights getting to know each other again. Caleb and Adey had a great relationship. I believe children pick up on the energy of their parents; Caleb was happy to see me happy. He smiled more, when he laughed it was Momma's rambunctious laughter coming out of Pop's mouth.

I often got anxious about how I was performing as a mother. It had gotten better with time; it had been a lot worse when Caleb was a baby. The first time I'd traveled for work, I'd spent the night in my hotel room crying. I was that mom, abandoning her child to be raised by other people while chasing a dream. Thankfully at the time, I didn't know the horrors to come, I didn't know I would sink so low, low enough to want to die and leave him behind.

In so many ways Caleb reminded me of Adey, he was put-together and wise beyond his years. I liked to think it was a result of the strong reaction of my blood to the blood of his father. I was worried about all the changes happening around him: moving to Claremont, his dad going to jail, and now Adey. Shade and Ebony insisted he'd be fine, Momma thought he needed the stability of a loving family, the kind of family I grew up in. I was proof that love ran deep, it seeped into the soul of the developing human and created roots so deep no storm could uproot them.

When Caleb was four, he fell while playing in the park. I was horrified and I guess he noticed because he looked at me and said, "I'm fine, Mommy." Stars shine brightest in the darkest nights, and Caleb was the star of the night that was my marriage to Richard.

I wasn't prepared for what sex would do to my relationship with Adey. It was like we broke the glass dividing our minds, and our souls melted into one. With Adey, there was only now. I didn't remember ever wanting so badly to be in the present.

Adey and I were stuck at the hip. I went on work trips with him, he became friends with the staff at my office. One day he walked in and the receptionist was holding out a Starbucks cup. She said with a bright smile, "Your regular."

He made a face like "Who told you I was coming?" She understood the look and responded without being asked, "It's Tuesday."

It had been Adey's idea to go on a trip to San Diego with Caleb, and we let him bring a friend as a treat. I was hoping Caleb would bond with a neighborhood girl and they would have a friendship like Adey and I did.

Shortly after we made the move to Claremont, Caleb became friends with Dwight, forcing me into a relationship with Dwight's mother, Mrs. Patterson. An eccentric TV agent who in many ways reminded me of Ms. Washington. From the stories I'd heard, she was the most cutthroat in the business. She had a reputation for being a no-nonsense woman, no matter how big the star. There was a story about a hotshot Disney princess she'd destroyed. The nineteen-year-old movie star had reportedly gotten high and thrown a tantrum on set. Mrs. Patterson made sure she never worked again.

Dwight would not have been my first choice for a friend, but as long as Caleb was happy, I was happy. Thankfully Ms. Patterson didn't turn us down when we asked if Dwight could go on the trip. She seemed happy to have him off her hands.

During the trip, I was pleasantly surprised to learn that Dwight was a well-behaved boy. I didn't know if it was a trend for children of dysfunctional adults to be so perfect or if Smith blood attracted these types.

The trip turned out splendid. Adey knew how to maintain the perfect balance, he made Caleb feel like a friend as opposed to forcing himself into the role of a dad. They went out camping during the trip, just the boys. I loved the idea, Caleb needed outdoors experience and I was okay with getting pampered all day. I had massages, ate hors d'oeuvres, and even had one of those pedicures where tiny fish eat the dead skin from your feet. I laughed through the whole thing.

Our cloud of bliss followed us back to Claremont. School was back in session and work was in full swing for Adey and me. A case at work threatened to break my peace, though. The first time I met this client, I walked into my office and saw this pretty biracial woman sitting in the guest chair. She sunk low in the chair like she was trying to disappear.

As she stretched out her hand to shake mine, I noticed the extra layers of concealer under her eyes, a bad attempt to hide the bruises. She noticed me staring too long and withdrew her hand, looking away.

"I need your help. I want a divorce from my husband." She paused and stared at me with teary eyes. "He is a monster."

I felt her pain, this had been me not long ago.

"He said if I leave, I get nothing. Not even my kids." She broke down in tears.

I learned that her husband had been abusing her. She'd signed a prenup and had no work. She wanted a way out for her and her kids.

When we were to meet up again to discuss the case, I waited for almost thirty minutes and she never showed up. When I finally got through to her phone, it was her husband telling me I was fired and they were staying together. I could swear I heard her sobbing in the background.

As angry as I was, Adey reminded me there was not much I could do if she was not willing to press charges. I let her know she could always come to me. Ebony and Shade suggested raising money for her, but I kicked against the idea, I found it invasive. I hoped she was okay; I worried about her.

To relax, Shade, Ebony, and I scheduled our annual girls' trip. After much deliberation, we decided to make it a couples' trip. Adey and I officially being a couple had swayed the decision. It was one of the best times of my life, the whole gang back together. I'm sure they could feel the love even in Kazakhstan. It was a blur of exotic fruits, bonfires by the beach, reminiscing, laughing. Adey was shocked when out of nowhere Shade looked him in the eyes, expression serious, and said, "You two belong together."

I smiled.

Ms. Washington came back from another trip on the eve of Thanksgiving. We had plans to have dinner with my parents. She joined us and showed up with too many gifts for Caleb; she spoiled him. In the middle of dinner, she abruptly said, "I think it's time for me to be Grannie Washington."

Adey burst out laughing but I was completely taken off guard. Yes, I loved Adey and Ms. Washington was a second mother to me, and I realized that I could handle her slight pressure. After noticing that I wasn't taking her seriously, Ms. Washington proceeded to other topics.

My Christmas present came in the form of good news; after numerous cycles of IVF, Shade and Johnny were finally expecting—twins. Only Shade could find a way to make something so tough seem easy. After her fifth miscarriage, she'd joked, "All hope isn't lost, if my eggs aren't working, I'll buy from my mother."

We laughed, but it was a morbid joke. That was Shade; there is something beautiful about a person that doesn't take life too seriously.

I told Shade and Ebony about Ms. Washington's comment, which they laughed off and said, "Why not? What are you and Adey waiting for anyway? It's been a few years since you journeyed back from hell."

Good news attracts more good news, because Eb also got pregnant that same month. That year was the biggest year for my firm since we'd opened. Adey got a job at UCLA, which meant he would stay in Southern California. Smith Construction landed a deal that allowed Pop to purchase a second construction property for a new branch of his business and Ms. Washington's book was on the New York Times Best Seller list.

Chapter 24

Adey stood by the window, phone receiver stuck to his ear. He had been on the phone for almost ten minutes. I knew something was going on because his voice broke whenever he responded. "I have work."

He stared out of the window.

"I'm sorry, I can't come."

He cut the call and turned to me.

"My dad."

It hit me like a ton of bricks—his dad had never reached out to him.

"He is sick, he wants me to visit."

It was a lot to take in.

"In Nigeria?" I asked.

Adey nodded. "Already told him I'm not going."

I was worried that Adey was making a hasty decision.

"You could give it a little more thought."

He shrugged and headed to the door. "Want a drink?"

At a time like this, he was thinking about me. I nodded. "Sure."

He left. I sat back and wondered what was going through Adey's mind. Most of us with ears in Nigeria followed the news, the stories of presidential scandal and the more horrifying stories of the crippling corruption in every level of government.

Then, there was the issue at hand, his dad. All his life, the man had been silent. Why now? How could he expect Adey to drop everything to hop on a plane because he'd said so? Did a critical illness absolve him of past wrongs?

I advised Adey to speak to Ms. Washington but he was worried that she might not take it well. Over the years Adey had solidified his position as Ms. Washington's protector. Before Ms. Washington got her own radio show, she'd been billed to be a guest host on a local TV talk show. According to her, the producer was "strung." He went into a blind rage and punched her square in the jaw. Adey filed a lawsuit that had bankrupted the studio. Ms. Washington purchased a Porsche.

Adey didn't speak about the call for a couple of days. I watched him carry on like nothing was wrong, but I could tell it was weighing heavily on his mind. I searched his face as we shared lunch in my office. I said a quick prayer and said.

"I think you should go."

He looked at me and shook his head.

"You know you want to. What if he dies?"

He shrugged!

"What difference does it make? He has been dead to me all these years."

He sounded like a hurt child. I put my arms around him and he relaxed a bit.

"People don't come back from the dead."

He got up to leave.

"I'll let you know about Boston."

He was changing to the topic; I smiled and nodded. Adey was to be honored by his alma mater as a rising star in the field of neurosurgery. He'd invited me as his plus-one to the ceremony. It was one of my proudest moments. Here he was, breaking stereotypes, showing the world that Black men could be successful. Adey succeeded in avoiding the topic of visiting Nigeria throughout our stay in Boston. I didn't bring it up, because I didn't want anything to ruin this moment for him. When we got back, we had dinner with Ms. Washington. I was shocked when he blurted out, "Dad wants to see me."

Ms. Washington choked on her wine. "Excuse me?"

He made an expression like it was a casual conversation. Ms. Washington cleared her throat like she was about to sing.

"Are you going?"

We held our breath, all three of us.

"I haven't decided."

Ms. Washington picked up her plate. "I think you should go, it's about time."

With that, she left the room.

After dinner Adey went to bed; I was unable to sleep so I took a walk in the garden. Who did I find? Ms. Washington, crying her eyes out. I sat with her without saying a word. I watched her cry.

"You raise a baby on your own and one day his father shows up and suddenly becomes 'Dad.'" A title he had not earned.

The pain was palpable. It didn't matter that Adey was a grown man in his thirties. She had raised her baby all alone and now his father was here for him. The way "Dad" had rolled off Adey's tongue made her furious.

Adey was undecided but I was personally looking forward to Nigeria. I let him know I was open to accompanying him. I hoped my decision to go on the trip would help him make up his mind. The last time I'd been in Africa, it was to purge my soul of the heartbreak of losing Adey. Now I was returning with him as my love. I filled Shade and Ebony in on the situation. It was like Shade had spent her whole life coming up with a list of stuff she wanted from Lagos. I was to find Ijebu garri—she was very specific, "Not the type they package for export, the local one that's sour."

I laughed. "Anything else?"

It wasn't a real question, but she answered anyway, "An ewedu broom, the one with hard bristles."

I laughed harder. All I could imagine as she was speaking was the face of the customs officers when I declared this voodoo-looking item in my luggage.

Johnny was keen on Lagos real estate, he said land was opening up in the Lekki Peninsula and the forecasts were promising. He was excited, and I had to remind them that the trip wasn't confirmed.

When Adey and I finally talked about his father's invitation, we were out at a theater downtown. We laid out the pros and cons of the trip.

"What if you never get this chance again?" I said.

Adey stared at a spot on the table. He nodded. "I hope I don't regret this."

I took his hand in mine; he lifted it up to his lips and kissed the back of my hand. "Thank you for coming with me."

Once we informed everyone of the dates of the trip, I placed a call to Oby, my Nigerian friend from college. Oby ran her own successful PR firm out of Lagos. She maintained a tight schedule but promised to make time to see me.

I'd met Oby sophomore year at UCLA. We were both psychology majors. Oby had come to school from Nigeria, her foreign student's tuition was fully paid. Oby's dad was part of the oil money clique. She wasn't extravagant, but it was clear money wasn't an issue.

The first time we met was at a friend's birthday dinner. It was her first real social gathering at the school. At the end of the dinner, Oby offered to pay the bill for the party of fifteen. She wanted to pay as a gift to the celebrant. I guess that was the way in Africa.

When I told Adey about Oby, he pointed out the similarities between us. As I gave him a rundown of Oby's upbringing, he commented, "Very similar to yours?"

I scoffed. "She grew up in Nigeria."

He replied with a calm certainty, "Her dad got rich and moved to Lagos, yours got rich and moved to Sunset Street."

I smiled.

"Hers got way richer."

Adey replied, "Who's counting?"

He was right. On campus, Oby and I were both in love with young men who were in faraway places. While my story experienced some hiccups, Oby's had gone smoothly. Once she was finished with her degree, she moved back to Nigeria and married the boy. I was excited at the idea of seeing her and she promised to help me acclimate to Nigeria.

I spent extra time with Caleb before the trip. We read stories and cuddled more. I knew Caleb would miss me, but he was perfectly fine with his grandparents. Ms. Washington had asked me to make sure Adey was okay.

Momma also had her moment. I was rummaging through her refrigerator, searching for dinner. She walked in and caught me with half of the cornbread in my mouth. I forced the entire thing down my throat.

She laughed and looked at me with a warmth that only Momma could muster. "Are you happy?"

I smiled, looked at her, and nodded. She smiled back.

"I know but I'm just checking. After all that happened, a mother needs to be sure . . ." Her voice trailed.

"I'm a really happy, Momma. Adey is Adey."

She smiled.

"You two were meant for each other."

She was right. It was the kind of love that heals. It was the kind of love she'd found with Pop.

The night before we were to leave, I kissed Adey and noticed he was trembling.

"My anxiety is through the roof."

Adey's anxiety was probably the fear of the unknown. All his life his father had been an abstract concept. A source of great emotional conflict. At this moment he was not Adey, the brilliant neurosurgeon. He was a wounded boy convinced that his father had never loved him and wouldn't love him now.

I held his hands and closed my eyes.

"Let us pray. Dear God, we thank you for our lives. We thank you for this opportunity to heal and grow. We ask that you lead us on this path and give Adey the wisdom and clarity of mind that he needs right now. Amen."

I opened my eyes; Adey was staring at me. He kissed me and whispered, "Thank you."

Chapter 25

As part of our route to Lagos, we had a layover in Dubai for about twenty-four hours. Adey and I decided to do a bit of exploring and the airline issued a transit visa. We visited the Sharjah Museum of Islamic Civilization, a stunning testament to the astronomical and artistic genius of the Islamic world. Artifacts at the museum dated as far back as the thirteenth century.

After that, we got pampered at a traditional spa. We were steamed with herbs and scrubbed with sugar. By the time we boarded our flight to Lagos, I was melted like butter.

On the flight, we played our usual travel "casting game," where we cast unsuspecting travelers in our make-believe movie. We cast the older pastor adjacent us in a sensational romantic drama. He was in a steamy relationship with the air hostess. His wife was deceased, so he wasn't exactly committing a sin, he was simply in love with a much younger girl. Adey and I laughed so hard.

I dozed off at some point during the flight and woke to the sound of the plane landing at Murtala Muhammed International Airport. We were finally in Lagos. The airport was chaotic, tons of people moving in different directions. Nothing was clear, the directional signs were mixed up. Adey and I followed the crowds till we arrived at the customs checkpoint, where I received my first shock of the welcome. The female customs officer gave me a funny look and asked, "What did you bring for us?"

Oby had warned me, but it was still jarring. I didn't know this woman, why was she expecting a gift from me? I smiled politely. She took my smile to mean I didn't understand.

"You don't have dollars?"

There was no shame in her game. I replied, "We aren't carrying cash."

She immediately became professional and stamped our passports. Adey laughed as we walked away, "She was about to whoop your ass."

We laughed. Thankfully, Oby's driver was waiting for us. We had a room booked at the George in Ikoyi, which was an hour, thirty-minute drive from the airport. I noticed the potbellied smiling man holding a sign that read Ade and Alero. Oby must have decided to write our names the Nigerian way. Lagos had its own rhythm. Music permeated the streets like a rooster in the morning dawn. The yellow-and-black painted buses buzzed with sounds. The motorcycles zipped between cars in tyrannical lyrics. Street hawkers gyrated to African gospel, fuji, and pop songs. Our driver, Mr. Okon, was verbose and didn't care if we were listening or not. He talked about electricity and how much he spent on petrol for his generator set. He spoke of the exchange rate and how one day he would own his own hundred-dollar bill. To Mr. Okon, the government and corruption were favorite topics that had the same end, "It is well." He let us know how lucky we were to live in America.

I was tempted to educate him on the circumstances that surrounded our becoming Black Americans or the true state of the Black person in America, but I sat in silence and listened to his story.

"Nigerians are dying, everybody wants to go to America, or Europe. But no way. All these bad people are carrying people through the desert and trading them as slaves."

His English was sprinkled generously with "broken English," aka pidgin. We heard details of a distant family member who'd tried migrating to Europe through the desert. His wife's brother's sister-in-law. Her dad had remarried shortly after her mom died. The new wife had no patience for a teenage daughter and beat her every chance she got. Soon the girl got a boyfriend and that's when the disaster began. Many believed that he was her pimp but no one was quite sure. She was fifteen years old. One night the family was robbed, every valuable was stolen. The next day, the girl vanished. Years later, she turned up shriveled, broken, and smelly. She recounted the harrowing journey in the desert, the ghosts and mirages that made men mad. She told stories of the men in the forests that could bend metals with their minds. She'd only made it as far as Libya. After some years of being sold to multiple owners, she was able to escape back to Nigeria. She died shortly after. This was the reason Mr. Okon had abandoned dreams of relocating. He ended that topic by saying, "If it is not with a visa and on a plane, count me out."

He moved on to the next topic but I had stopped listening as I thought of the poor slave girl who'd jumped from frying pan to fire. I looked out of the window as we weaved through the Ikeja traffic. We passed the Third Mainland Bridge, which resembled the freeways in the United States.

The island was a bit different from the mainland. It was less congested and had much taller and more modern buildings. The pace there was slower and people seemed a bit more relaxed. It felt like I was in a suburb in the United States. Driving down Osborne, it was very clear we were in the affluent part of town. Mr. Okon pointed out the estates, naming them like we had a clue, "Here is Dolphin, Osborne, Parkview." He was happy to serve as a de facto tour guide.

Once we checked into our room, we placed a call to Adey's father. Adey's father lived in his home state of Osun. Adey informed him that we would be spending some time in Lagos before making the trip to Ile-Ife. The old man didn't sound excited, but there wasn't much he could do. I agreed with Adey's plan to make good memories in Lagos in case the visit with his dad went awry. We were hopeful the trip would be a great experience, but we had a contingency plan.

Dinner that night was by the pool and we decided to try something familiar. Adey and I had jollof rice with chicken and plantains. It was delicious. Later during the trip, at Mr. Okon's insistence, we tried jollof rice from a local buka and I must say, street food speaks the same language in every country. The conversation at the buka was as exciting as the food. A group of men sat debating the Nigerian Civil War. One of the men argued that the war was important to stop an insurgence that had been threatening to divide the country, while the other thought that it was a genocide of a group of people fighting for independence. The female owner of the buka, Madam K as she was called, spoke about the war being a battle for oil and control of the south. Madam K said with a sigh,

"When two elephants fight, it is the ground that suffers." The ground was the 1.3 million Biafran children who were killed during the war. On May 30, 1967, four days after the Eastern Region had voted to secede from Nigerian, Ojukwu announced an independent Biafra, made up of the eastern states and oil-rich South. The Nigerian army declared war on July 6. I read later that Britain and Russia supplied the Nigerian army with ammunition while France funded Biafra. Two years and six months after the war began, Nigeria celebrated on the graves of Biafran dreams.

At some point the conversation in the buka became so heated, I worried a fight might break out. Mr. Okon told me the participants in the argument were from the same tribe. In his words, "They are from the same place; they will speak their language and settle. No fight here. They are happy."

Nigeria has over five hundred languages yet the word that came to mind was an Afrikaans term, *geluksalig*, which describes a state of happiness. Not the transient excitement that comes with a new purchase or good news. It describes a divinely inspired joy. A joy that the creators of the language must have experienced. I wondered if the happiness Mr. Okon mentioned was sustainable in such conflicted environment.

We stood in the most populous Black nation in the world; never in my life had I been so comfortably Black. It was impossible to not love myself when all around me I saw a luminous reflection of my blackness. I wondered what Grandpa would have felt being here, in Lagos. My imaginative mind was creating a magical utopia. A world without the need to fight for rights. We would come ready-made with a love for ourselves and others. Being home reminds you that you are not alone. In Lagos, I felt my spirit amplified, healing generations of pain. Adey also seemed lighter; I could see the city's effect on him. As a Black neurosurgeon, Adey had to fight extra hard for respect in his field. Being a Black man in America means being in a constant state of fight or flight. Fight to stay alive, to be free, and to be taken seriously. In Nigeria, the battle was about the soul of the nation. A wrestle against the imprints of division left by the colonists. There were fights in both worlds but in the latter, we were part of a national tribe while the isolation of the former fragmented the soul.

Nigeria—the giant of Africa, with over 200 million and counting. It is said that one in every four Africans is Nigerian. Nigeria is a promise that keeps finding a reason to prolong her coming of age. God is ever present there.

I found myself praying and I was not the only one. On every street corner, there was a church or a mosque. On our first Sunday in Lagos, Adey and I were invited to church by Oby. It was very common to get invited to church in Nigeria. Halfway through praise and worship, I saw a young woman, couldn't be more than twenty-nine years old. She got down on her knees, totally oblivious to those around her when she broke down in tears. She sang the words to the song and her pain was palpable. I knelt down and prayed that she would get relief from her struggles.

I woke up bright and early on Monday morning with a sense of purpose. I decided to go down to breakfast and have a few minutes of me time. When I was done eating, the waiter brought the bill. I looked at it and my heart jumped. Two thousand five hundred for some pancakes and eggs! Their printer didn't have the naira symbol, it printed the amount with a dollar sign.

"Is this accurate?"

The dark-skinned waiter leaned in for a closer look and declared, "Yes, ma."

I tried to hide my panic. I wasn't cheap, I'd been blessed in life. But $2,500 for breakfast was a bit steep.

"Is this dollars or naira?" I inquired.

"Two thousand five hundred naira, ma."

"Ha!" I laughed.

"Yes, ma."

I explained that I'd thought it was dollars. He laughed and shook his head.

There was a time it had been one dollar to a naira. Those times were long gone, the gap between the dollar and naira had widened considerably. In most African countries you could spend seven figures on a car. A N20,000 dress, N1,500 on a cocktail. The figures were mind-numbing. Adey became our currency converter. Every time we heard a naira price, Adey would quickly convert it to the corresponding dollar amount. Each time, I would sigh in relief. We were in traffic and I saw a man handing five naira to a beggar. I was not in any way judging, but I had to wonder, what would five naira do for this woman hawking on a the roadside with a tray of bananas on her head, a toddler yanking her skirt and a baby on her back? It was a common occurrence, from the women hawking on the streets to the ones in shop stalls. The entire place was packed with babies. Babies on backs, babies playing in the muddy puddles in the street. Half-dressed children searching through heaps of trash for anything that could be reclaimed. I felt helpless and I admired these women. These strong women breaking their backs in the hot Nigerian sun.

"I am concerned about the education of these women."

Mr. Okon laughed and said, "Aunty, na so all of us be na, I don become man, I no die."

This was the pidgin way of saying that he'd grown up in the same environment and turned out okay.

I have no evidence to prove this, but I believe pidgin language originated in Nigeria. Every country in West Africa claims ownership of pidgin. The West African pidgin gave birth to the Jamaican Patios, and other broken-down forms of English spoken mostly by Blacks. Everyone has their own twist on it. I'll never forget a conversation Adey had with a northern man at the Bureau de Change.

"Oga, I no go lie for me, na so we dey do am for here, I go ask around, I come back, see say na the same thing."

Mr. Okon had translated it to mean: "Sir, I am giving you a fair price; you can ask around and come back."

I would never have guessed that in a million years. I decided to learn some pidgin while in Lagos.

Chapter 26

O by's house was a sprawling mansion located in the heart of Banana Island, a settlement recently created on sand-filled land at the edge of Ikoyi. The late chief Adeleke had planned to develop some land in the Victoria Island area of the city but his land had been reclaimed by the government. He was then offered new land in compensation. His vision was to create an island, completely sufficient, with its own airport. Many were shocked when Adeleke proceeded to dredge the coast of Ikoyi. He hired world-class architects to create his masterpiece. Sadly, the government showed up again, the project was claimed, and the sand was dumped in the shape of a banana, which is how it ended up with the name Banana Island. A house here cost anywhere from $300,000 to $3 million. It was billed as a prime area for real estate investment in the coming years.

When we were at school, Oby talked about parties and the outrageous lives of the Nigerian elite. She talked about the Adekoyas and Gbadamosis, who'd recently made it big in politics, and how the wives threw lavish parties. She spoke of the president's wife, who'd died during a cosmetic surgery. The stories of corruption and misuse of the national funds for personal gain presented a dichotomy in a nation with high rate of poverty. She also told us a much lesser-known story of a female senator who was building her own wealth through illegal weapons. Lagos elites wore and drove their wealth. It was clear their ultimate motivation was to show how much wealth they could amass, with little sense of service or legacy.

Oby's house was a testament to nouveau riche opulence. The living room furniture had heavy gold trims. There were pillars in the house and sculptures made to mimic Michelangelo's works. Oby's husband was loud and funny. Her kids were at boarding school in the UK, in line with the preference of the Nigerian elite. Most wealthy Nigerians sent their children away to boarding schools, a legacy of colonization. The desire to replicate the English way of life was part of the blueprint left in Nigeria. Oby lived like a duchess. When we arrived for dinner, a uniformed butler brought out bottles of Cristal and Dom Perignon. The appetizer table was laded with caviar, crème fraîche, lemon wedges, hard-boiled eggs (yolks and whites chopped separately), mini potatoes, minced onions, blinis, and triangles of toast lightly coated with unsalted butter. I asked Oby why there were no Nigerian delicacies and she led us to other side of the room, where she introduced us to the other spread before us. There was an assortment of plantain fritters, suya (spicy skewered beef), Nigerian spring rolls, meat and fish pies, chin-chin, puff-puff, scotch eggs, akara or black-eyed pea fritters, and much more.

Oby's husband was a successful businessman who imported everything from toothpicks to baby shoes to heavy machinery. He and Adey were engrossed in conversation, which meant that Adey liked the guy. Oby gave me a tour of the mansion, complete with a massive closet that held Hermès bags and Chanel pearls. We overheard Nnamdi tell Adey, "All I want in this life is to spoil my wife and enjoy life."

After the statement, he laughed like he had just shared the most intriguing secret. This was the story of Naija men. We'd learned from Mr. Okon that everything Nigerian was referred to as Naija. The name packed a punch like the overhand right of a seasoned boxer. That one word captured the essence of the people's alertness to opportunities to make knockout moves. Naija men wanted to impress and take care of their queens. It was African love. You saw it everywhere from the young to elderly. The long walks on starry Nigerian nights to whispers in the dark spaces without NEPA—the National Electric Power Authority distributed electricity at will. Love bred within the chaos of the country. It was like the flower that springs up in desert places.

But the media only magnified crooks who extorted money from old ladies and lonely single women searching for love on matchmaking sites.

An example I'd heard was a fifty-two year old single Californian, Barbara, who fell head over heels in love with "Edward" from Chicago. A few weeks into their relationship, Edward hit a rough patch and asked her for a few hundred dollars to pay some bills. She sent it because it was Edward. She knew him and they were in love. It turned out Edward was in a rut and the bad news kept coming. By the third month, she noticed she had spent over $5,000 on him. Would she have to take out a second mortgage on her home? Should she dip into her daughter's college fund? It didn't matter because Edward was the best man she had ever known. Soon he would visit and they would live happily ever after. After she paid for his plane ticket, Edward went silent for two painful months. He reappeared and informed her that his real name was John and he was from Nigeria. His mea culpa was that although this had started out as a scam, he hadn't planned to fall in love and had chosen to confess. He told her heartbreaking stories of personal losses and how the past months had healed him. The intensity of his stories pulled her ever so much closer to John. She forgave him and leaned into this love. So began the process of getting John to America. It involved building a home for his parents in the village, paying for passports, and bribing officials. After six grueling years, Barbara filed for bankruptcy and John disappeared from her life. She hired a detective, who traced John to Onitsha. He lived in the house she'd built for him with his wife and four children. What a heart-wrenching story, and John should be prosecuted to the full extent of the law. Barbara would never be the same again and would continuously repeat her war story about Nigerian men. However, in a country of millions of people, half of whom were men, a few people's crimes shouldn't taint the rest of the nation. I was grateful that Adey and Nnamdi were representing the good guys. Nigerian men loved and built up their women. Oby explained that her and Nnamdi would be traveling to London in the morning but she would connect me with a tour guide who would definitely make our stay fun. She took a sip of her peach green tea drink, moved closer, and whispered, "No one knows Lagos like Fola. You will thank me later."

Oby was very health-conscious and only fed her body with goodness. Adey and I made a decision at that party to pause our alcohol intake while in Nigeria. The truth was that we'd been consuming more than usual in the past few years. Right there at Oby's party, I decided to stick to water.

Fola's energy was palpable and his exuberance contagious. The call came from the front desk that we had a visitor in the lobby. Fola was waiting for us in his luminosity. He wore fluorescent-green tights and a baggy coral-pink crop top. Fola noticed me staring and promptly added, "I know what you are thinking. No, I'm not gay but I'd have no problem being one."

I liked him already. A square peg in a round hole, Fola had forged his own space in this ultraconservative system where religion and culture were peas in a pod. The day's itinerary was the beach and we dressed accordingly. Fola completed his look with a royal-blue-and-gold mariachi hat. It turned out he didn't mean one particular beach but five. We went to five beach fronts off Eti-Osa.

Fola's tales of Bar Beach spiritual ceremonies are worth repeating. It was widely believed that a temperamental sea goddess, Yemoja, inhabited the waters there. Fishermen and sailors sought her blessings because she was the protector of all who traveled on water. She was the patron deity of women and especially pregnant women. People flocked to the sea at night to appease Yemonja. She attended to only those who sought out her blessings. It was the reason many arrived there at night seeking her blessings. There was a story told of a woman who came to the beach with her children for a Sunday picnic. Without warning, the waves swept the baby she was holding away. All hope was lost but this woman all of a sudden stopped crying and summoned Yemoja to bring her baby back. Within a minute, the waves had brought the baby back and the astonishment was that the baby was alive. The goddess of Bar Beach, however, was about to get a makeover. There were rumors that the coast was to be filled in to create a new city. Oby informed us that he'd heard this from a client, who'd heard from a top Nigerian businessman that new land was opening up off the coast of Victoria Island.

We found out that Fola was a lawyer licensed to practice in Nigeria and the UK. He had a master's degree from Leeds. He spoke seven languages, including three major Nigerian languages. As he so aptly put it, his passion was enjoyment. He had definitely created a niche for himself as a Lagos luxury expert.

Fola and Adey got off to a rocky start. Adey found his brashness off-putting. Adey whispered before we got into the car, "Do we really need him?"

I told him to give Fola a chance, however Adey's reaction made me wonder if he was threatened by another man's freedom of expression. I decided it was best to discuss this another time and I brought it up when we got back to the hotel, "Do you dislike Fola because you think he is gay?"

"Hell no, I have nothing against gay people. Do you know what he said to me?"

I was curious, "What did he say?"

He faked Fola's English accent the best he could, "'If you don't take care of her, I have men that will kick you to curb and make her their queen.' Imagine that!"

I laughed so hard. He teased me, "Oh, you wanna be a . . . what did Nnamdi call 'em?"

The name he was looking for was *runs girl*. Underneath the glitz and glam of the Lagos luxury life was an unseen economy. There were hushed conversations in parties, contracts awarded and deals signed in the name of sex. The postcolonial Nigerian woman was fierce. All around me, I saw educated women, executives, entrepreneurs, and movers and shakers. Women were rewriting rules and creating legacies. However, there were also some women who applied their influence in the bedrooms of the "big boys." It had become a normative practice. Men gifting houses, cars, businesses, contracts, even government appointments to women who were eye candy. At a particular gathering, a woman seated next to me gossiped about a lady who had recently been promoted to lead one of the top banks in Lagos.

"See how she is carrying her shoulder? Like we don't know that she got her appointment because she slept with a minister."

I pretended like I wasn't listening but she didn't care. She was immersed in her tale and was soon joined by others. I got tired of the negative commentary and went out to the balcony for some fresh air. On the balcony, I ran into a group of men smoking Indian hemp. It was a curious sight because they were dressed flamboyantly in agbadas. Why was Lagos looking more like Los Angeles? I cringed.

A lot had changed since the silent Adey years, as I now referred to them. I was there with Adey, the love of my life, at the beach in Lagos, and had no need of a joint. Life was good. The sun was setting and the crescent moon was visible in the sky. The sunset gave the clouds a fiery purple glow.

Adey and I laughed at the absurdity of the people pouring salt water and oil on a car they were sacrificing to God while they had to stand in the burning heat. We laughed at memories of yesteryear. We laughed about Mr. Okon's stories. We laughed till our tummies hurt. Then we ate hot suya and drank Fanta. We paid dearly for all that food we ate—both Adey and I had the runs that night. It was during what felt like my hundredth trip to the toilet, at about nine that night, that I had my first experience with a NEPA blackout. I was sitting there, coaching myself through the pain, when all of a sudden it was pitch-black. A hotel employee was at our door in minutes, informing us that both the main and backup generators were faulty but would be up and running in a few minutes. Generators were how Nigerians powered their lives; the country's electricity company was completely incompetent. They still had not figured out how to provide enough electricity for the entire nation. This meant that rolling blackouts were common occurrences. Every cluster of buildings that went dark in Lagos was accompanied by a chorus of generators. I saw generators as big as minivans and some as small as a traveling bag. You could be sitting in a restaurant and boom! Everything shut down. Everyone acted like it was business as usual. The steady hum of a generator was a welcome sound.

Nigerians were resilient! The average family had to pay light bills *and* fuel a generator. I worried about how much small businesses lost every day on petrol and generator maintenance. I worried about the impact of the lack of electricity had on the development of a nation. For many people, like Mr. Okon, the lack of electricity in Nigeria had been a case of life and death. Mr. Okon had lost a sister during childbirth. She was in her home when she went into labor, her husband spent over thirty minutes navigating traffic. At the hospital, the doctors said the baby was breech and was wheeled into an emergency C-section. Halfway through the procedure, the lights went out and the backup generators malfunctioned. By the time light was restored at the hospital, his sister was dead from internal bleeding, leaving a husband and young son behind.

Chapter 27

I t was Fola's idea to visit Abuja and Port Harcourt in an effort to complete the trio of Nigerian mega cities. Abuja was a sharp contrast to Lagos. It was not as congested and there was semblance of community planning, with wide roads, functional street lights, a beautiful airport. I felt my lungs expand as I inhaled the clean air, purified by the altitude. Abuja was the first planned city to be built in Nigeria, 1,180 feet above sea level, **and ha**d a cooler climate and less humidity than we'd found in Lagos. The city had a strange coldness, it was as though the presence of the seat of government robbed it of its humanity. I wanted to go sightseeing, but Fola got us invited to a networking party.

At the party, we met elegant Muslim women covered in gold-threaded hijabs, wearing perfumes from the most exclusive merchants in Arabia. The host glistened like Princess Jasmine. Her caramel skin shone under the lights. She wore dark eyeliner and a complex ring that extended from her nose to her ear. Her hands were covered in the intricate patterns of henna, there known as Lalle. Her baby-blue hijab was almost transparent, so we could see her curly hair packed into a bun. The hijab had a network of gold patterns around the edges, these merged with the gold trimmings on her royal-blue abaya. Her gold bracelets clinked as she moved her hands. Apparently, she was about to get a seat on the UN council. The party was just like its host, larger than life. The attendees laughed and sang, all the while discussing the future of the country. Adey and I felt out of place but very blessed to be there. Adey saw it as a sign that Nigeria was welcoming him home with open arms.

On the trip to Port Harcourt, Adey and I got into an argument about his decision to give his mother the silent treatment. It was our first argument and it was more exhausting than I could have anticipated. Shortly after we landed, Ms. Washington had started acting very needy of Adey. She complained that Adey hadn't called once since we'd landed in Lagos. She was upset with him for letting Celia take a week off. Ms. Washington was meant to be in Germany for a speaking engagement. Celia's daughter was in sophomore in college and they had not seen each other in months. Seeing as Adey and Ms. Washington were both out of town, Adey had given her a week off to see her daughter. Ms. Washington had returned early to an empty house. Adey decided that the most effective response was the silent treatment. My attempts at reconciliation of mother and son did not yield any results, so I left him alone. I could see the stubborn streak but it only made me smile. A man was entitled to his decisions especially when it had to do with his mother.

When we arrived in Port Harcourt, we stayed at a hotel in Old Government Reserved Area, home to the state Government House. We were told that Port Harcourt was the fifth-largest city in Nigeria, after Lagos, Kano, Ibadan, and Benin City. It was also one of the country's national ports. I wondered why Nigeria still maintained colonial identifiers. For example, Port Harcourt had been named for Lewis Harcourt, once a colonial secretary. Why not conduct a national renaming campaign so we could bear our own identifiers? I'd come to speak as a Nigerian. It turned out that I was 40 percent Nigerian according to the DNA test that Fola had encouraged us to take. Adey was 55 percent Nigerian. So this was also my home and this sense of belonging felt like wearing comfortable pajamas.

One night, we went out with Fola to a local bar to enjoy palm wine and the local favorite, fresh fish. A fight broke out barely thirty minutes after our arrival. The owner of the bar was being held back by some of her staff and a few regulars. It wasn't an easy task, she was a big woman, a sharp contrast to her lanky husband, the object of her fury. The couple had been together for over fifteen years. In that time the husband had been unable to hold a job and they had five children to feed. I gathered that he was also an unrepentant drunk who had at least four other children with various women. On this particular day, he had broken into her safe and stolen money to give his latest girlfriend. She was so angry. We were scared and wanted to leave but Fola assured us that we were safe. The man apologized and left the canteen but Fola told us later he never returned the money. His wife simply learned to move the safe to another location. Marriages like that existed here. They were functional but without intimacy. She stayed so that her children didn't suffer, the damage of a divorce not being worth the pursuit in her opinion. By the end of the evening, all appeared to be well in the world. Adey and I laughed when we saw the restaurant owner serve her delinquent husband pepper soup, a local delicacy, essentially a bowl of meat or fish, some spices, water, and hot pepper.

The man seated at the table beside us noticed Adey and I laughed. He shook his head and said in pidgin, "Na why people no suppose put mouth for husband-and-wife matter."

"Hear, hear!" Another responded.

We took a trip to the coastal town of Degema, a picturesque city in the south of Rivers State. As we stood at the waterside by old colonial buildings, Adey asked if we could delay the trip to Osun State. He was obviously anxious. I suggested that he wait till we returned to Lagos to make a decision. We spent the day exploring the town and marveling at the buildings made of periwinkle shells. The people here lived off the sea. The entire town was littered with all sorts of shells. Shells formed the pavement of the roads, they sat in heaps for children to play. We had a meal of the most delicious barbecued fish. I wanted to savor each bite of the hot, sizzling croaker, which had a rich, fresh earthy taste brought on by the incorporation of herbs. I asked for another serving.

Driving through Rivers State was a reflection of Nigeria in its contradictions. A land that produced so much wealth was in ruins. Completely decimated by greed. I wasn't prepared for what we saw in Ogoniland. Films of death lay over miles and miles of rivers turned into graveyards. This place was left desolate, stripped of all goodness, and the land left to die. The people lived in mud huts. All around the villages, we saw children with swollen bellies, hair turned brown from malnutrition. It was the aftershock of a seismic colonial greed helped along by shortsighted Nigerians. Fola told of an incident in a village in Delta State where a local refinery exploded and over eighty lives were lost. The government's move to clamp down on bunkering operations was breeding a monster. A monster that would show its head in the coming years as militancy rendered the region useless.

We returned to Lagos in reflective moods. Fola was back in his element and his voice returned to its usual pitch. He proceeded to present his detailed Lagos tour plans. We started out with the Lekki Art Market, nestled in a ghetto in the new, developing Lekki axis with rows and rows of handcrafted work. Adey was tempted to purchase a lion hide; the seller claimed that he had traveled to the forests of Kogi and shot the lion himself. He told us a very elaborate story of how he'd narrowly escaped with his life and ended up flaying the lion with a sharp stick. He'd then apparently survived alone in the jungle for three days living off lion meat. I was turned off by the poaching. Adey concluded that it was overpriced and that he couldn't help feeling for the lion. However I purchased something for everyone in my life—Ankara-print baby clothes for Shade, Ankara dresses for both Shade and Ebony, a handcrafted elephant husk for Pop, a multicolor necklace for Ms. Washington, a silk scarf for Momma, and a white embroidered top for Caleb. The streets of Lagos Island reminded me of New York—tall buildings that threatened to spill onto the road and the constant flow of human traffic. The whole place felt like one huge market, at every turn there was someone selling something. All that was missing were huge billboards in Tinubu Square.

This boat ride at sunset was breathtaking. Adey held me as we watched the sun disappear in a haze of orange. I rocked gently in his arms to the sound of gusting winds. I felt alive and hoped he felt it too. I watched as the water glided against the boat in a lover's tide. Soon darkness set in Lagos and the stars came out to play. We joked about the idea of life in Lagos. One could easily get intoxicated with the idea of permanence on a night like this.

From there, we went what Fola called restaurant hopping. We visited at least thirteen of the most exclusive hot spots in Lagos. I never want to see an isi-ewu bowl again. When the chef said "goat's head," I was curious but when a pair of goat's eyes stared at me, I quickly left the table. That moment began my vow to never eat meat. I became a vegetarian in Lagos.

The next day, Adey decided it was time to make the trip to Ile-Ife.

Chapter *28*

"Don't tell Adey, but his mom collapsed and we are on the way to the hospital."

Momma's call knocked the wind out of me. How was I supposed to keep something like this from Adey? Ms. Washington was like a mother to me and I definitely couldn't continue with this day pretending like nothing was happening. I hadn't had much experience with death, I'd carefully avoided imagining life without my parents. Accepting that your loved ones will also get older and die is a scary notion. The prayer of any parent is to be buried by their children, not the other way around. I don't think parents realize that no kid wants to bury a parent either.

I was anxious and didn't know what to do with myself. I avoided Adey by going for a swim and felt a bit better. I spent an hour on the phone with Caleb; he told me about a new friend he'd made in chess club. Caleb had been born with a brain for chess, a good trait he'd inherited from his father. At five he was beating Pop in games and now he was almost a chess master, competing across the state. I worried that his love for chess would make him a target for bullies. Kids could be really mean. He proved to me I had nothing to worry about because he rode this chess wave admirably. He also loved being smart.

Finally, I got a call that Ms. Washington was stable. I sat on the bed with Adey as I broke the news to him, "Your mom collapsed."

He got up alarmed. "What?"

"She is stable now. I didn't want to tell you until I was sure everything was okay."

He stared at me. "You should have told me."

I responded, "I didn't want you to worry. There was nothing you could have done from here."

He sighed and sat back on the bed. "I stopped talking to her and this happened."

I noticed his hand was shaking and squeezed it gently.

"It is not your fault."

It truly wasn't his fault. The doctors said it was a combination of high blood pressure, dehydration, and exhaustion. Ms. Washington had imagined the worst and thought she had cancer. The doctors ordered her to slow down, which was a tall order for Ms. Washington. She lived quite a hectic lifestyle. Her days were a blur of cameras, lights, makeup, airplanes, hotel rooms, and performances. In the last five years, she had not been in one country longer than a month.

Two days before our trip to Osun, I saw Adey quietly sobbing in the bathroom. It was probably a combination of what had happened with his mother and anxiety from the impending meeting with his dad. There is something sexy and reassuring about a man who is in touch with his emotions. I freshened up and left the room to grant him time alone. Childhood trauma is pervasive. As we become adults, we are forced to bury the wounded child and become functional adults. A perfectly adjusted adult is expected to flourish on the soil of a broken spirit. Most times our inner child is just there, beneath the surface, crying to be heard. Coupled with the constant absence of his mother, Adey hadn't had a childhood because he'd been parentified. He had always cared for his mother and was parentified. I hoped he would get through this.

I decided to get my hair braided to give Adey some space. There was no better time than this to conquer the herculean task. I had booked this appointment, which was in walking distance from the hotel, via Mr. Okon's recommendation. No one had warned me about sanitation day, though. In Lagos, there was a day set aside for cleaning once a week. The normally busy streets were deserted till about 10:00 a.m. I was walking down to the shop when I was accosted by two uniformed officers. Other people were standing around in doorways so I wondered what I had done wrong.

"Wetin you dey find for here?"

I looked around to be sure the question was directed at me.

"Wetin you dey find? No be you I dey follow talk?"

His comment confirmed my fears, I was in some sort of trouble. The Nigerian police were notorious for corruption. I'd heard horrid stories of commercial bus drivers being shot and killed for twenty- and fifty-naira bribes. Not even up to a dollar. Here I was, standing face-to-face with the dreaded police.

"Good morning, officer," I said, in the most Nigerian accent I could muster. And they burst out laughing. Out of fear I laughed with them.

"You for tell us na you be JJC."

JJC was an acronym for "Johnny Just Come," a term used to describe those of us who were new to the ways of Nigeria. I nodded earnestly, how would I have told them when we'd only just started our conversation?

"Person for tell you before you commot house, today na sanitation."

I guess the other officer understood my confusion from the way I furrowed my brow. He added, "Sanitation, no movement, we clean."

He spoke like he was talking to someone who didn't understand English.

"I am so sorry, I didn't know."

The first officer spoke again, this time in what I'm assuming was intended to be an American accent.

"Now 'ur gonna do somering for us. We gorra le you go."

This was familiar, I'd experienced it when I went to use the bathroom at the airport when we landed. The cleaner stood by smiling as I washed my hands. She unhygienically unwrapped the roll of tissue paper and handed me a piece. I cleaned my hands and thanked her. She smiled and said, "Ma, do something for me, four months now they have not paid us."

She was happy when I handed her a five-dollar bill. Here I was again but this time I had naira notes. I dipped my hands in my pocket and brought out a couple of N200 notes. I handed them to the men. They smiled and thanked me. The quiet officer added, "Go siddon one place o, make another patrol squad no catch you."

With that, they walked away.

An hour later the woman showed up and five hours after that we were done. Looking at my reflection in the mirror, I felt proud to be here. The braid met at a point on the top of my head, giving me an instant face-lift.

Adey was pacing the reception when I returned. I'd accidentally left without a phone. When he had gotten out of the bathroom and noticed I was gone, he'd assumed I'd be right back. But as the hours went by, fear of the unknown crept in. I felt bad adding to his already tense day. The good news was that he loved the hair and jokingly asked if we could fly the hairdresser to the US. That night we went on the most romantic date. After dinner we sat on a rock at the beach, watching the full moon. Our peace was periodically broken by the shouting coming from a prayer squad in white attire some distance away.

Adey was on the phone with Ms. Washington every other hour once she got discharged. He made it a point to call her repeatedly throughout the day, especially because she had convinced us to finish our trip and not hurry back. The bond between Ms. Washington and Adey was something I hoped to someday have with Caleb. I liked to believe we were off to a right start.

It was finally time to head to Osun. Fola was acting like we were never coming back. He showed up early at the hotel and kept tapping on the door as if it were a drum. I ignored it but the tapping increased in volume and intensity. Adey also stirred in his sleep and I envied how he could sleep through noise.

I opened the door and Fola hugged me, lamenting hysterically. The noise was enough to wake Adey up.

"Oh my God! My fave couple is leaving me."

I managed a laugh as he pulled himself off me. "You know we are coming back to Lagos, right? It's just for a couple of days."

He rolled his eyes, in his usual Fola way and said, "Are you saying you won't miss me?"

Adey and I mumbled our responses as affectionately as possible. He looked at me like he was just seeing me for the first time.

"Love your hair."

That was the random, self-absorbed, over-the-top Fola that we had come to love. Fola was the kind of person you fell in love with instantly. I'd seen the protective side of Fola during what felt like our millionth trip to the market. I was trudging behind, all the while staring at the floor to avoid getting my feet in the muddy puddles and trash that covered the street. Suddenly I was pulled by a rough peddler.

"Fine Aunty, come buy."

I wasn't prepared for the sheer force of the pull and I landed butt down in a puddle that was turning green at the edges. Fola saw red. In an instant, Fola was transformed into a weird super-Nigerian version of himself. His veins bulged in his neck as he screamed a tirade of pidgin words. The next thing I knew, he had the guy in a choke hold and I was holding him back, begging for the peddler's life. A small crowd was building and I had a feeling they weren't on our side.

Later, Oby told me that Fola's reaction had been foolish because everyone knew you didn't fight in the market. However I'd found it delightful to see him spring into action. Fola asked if we wanted him to accompany us to Ife-Ife; we told him we would be okay. Adey and I concluded that Fola was best in wine shops in the heart of Old Ikoyi or the clubs in Victoria Island. Osun would be a different phase of our trip.

Chapter *29*

M r. Okon wasn't his usual chatty self on the drive to Ile-Ife, but after a bit of prodding, he revealed that his daughter had malaria and now his wife had come down with typhoid and malaria. Adey was concerned because malaria kills millions of Africans every year. We were even more concerned that people were self-diagnosing or being misdiagnosed. Mr. Okon reassured us they'd been tested. When we asked why he wasn't home taking care of his family, he said his wife preferred that he was out hustling. His wife and daughter were being cared for by family because they couldn't afford any extra doctor fees.

Mr. Okon's mood got better as we left Lagos and he proceeded to purchase everything that was hawked in traffic. He bought bread and groundnuts, boiled guinea fowl eggs, which I suspected were going bad because Adey and I had to roll down the windows to get rid of the smell. Adey was also a lot more animated than I'd expected. We would get through whatever was waiting for us in Ile-Ife. I didn't know why we'd waited this long. I imagined what would have been if Adey and I had allowed ourselves to be together from the start or if I had never met Richard. The only shining light that came out of that dark period was Caleb. I knew that I loved Adey in a way that defied words. I loved the way he loved me. I would have gone to the ends of the earth for him. I hoped this love didn't crush me. As we rode in silence through the dusty roads of Ibadan, Adey held my hand and looked me in the eyes. He said, "I love you, Allie Pooh."

It was so random and perfect. Adey was a location in space and time; in Adey-world I was ten years old and thirty years old simultaneously. I was in Nigeria and strolling down Sunset Street. Location and time had collided in Nigeria. We had entered the thin place where time was irrelevant.

We decided against sightseeing in Ibadan. We however tried an amala spot that came highly recommended by Fola. The seller sat on a small stool in front of a large pot of a tomato-based stew that had parts of meat floating freely in it. When I say parts, I mean all the parts. I spotted lungs, skin, intestines. One thing all Nigerians have in common is that they do not waste their meat. As long as it can be cooked, it can be eaten. Okon was vehemently anti-amala. His refusal to eat amala was a form of protest against becoming fully Yorubanized. He was an Efik man fully acculturated, including speaking Yoruba fluently, but he drew a line at amala.

Fola was right about the place. It was one of the best meals that I'd eaten since I'd landed in Nigeria, for less than a fraction of the cost of all the meals we'd eaten put together. The amala felt like hot, soft balls easing down my throat, perfectly wrapped in ewedu and gbegiri soup. I watched as Adey struggled with a piece of goat meat. It was hard to stay awake the rest of the way. Mr. Okon begged us repeatedly to stay awake since he was also struggling. To help his cause, he turned up the volume on the radio as Fela Anikulapo Kuti's voice filled the car. I couldn't sleep anymore as my body moved to the beat, "Zombie o, Zombie . . . A joro, jara, joro."

Mr. Okon lavished us with stories about Calabar people. **Efik people came from Calabar, the** capital of Cross River State, in southeastern Nigeria, and one of the oldest trading centers in Nigeria. The city was set on a natural hill overlooking the Calabar River. Calabar had been established as a center of slave trade by the British in seventeenth century, something Mr. Okon didn't like to mention, but history cannot be erased. He told us that Calabar women were naturally elegant and wore long Victorian-looking dresses with dramatic hairstyles, adorned with combs and mirrors. He narrated what had happened to him when he saw the cost for his wife's onyonyo, the traditional dress used for their traditional marriage ceremony. But when she flowed towards him in a fluid dance, moving her shoulders the tribal way, he knew he had made the right choice.

Finally, we arrived at Ile-Ife after over three hours on the road. The inscription at the entry to the town read "Ile-Ife. Here is the cradle of the Yoruba race." We were excited to be a part of it. We had researched and understood the importance of this place. According to traditional history, the Yoruba civilization began in Ife-Ife and it was the location where the gods descended to earth. The name, Ile-Ife, literally means "place of dispersion." According to Yoruba tradition, Ife was founded by the deities Oduduwa and Obatala when they created the world. Obatala fashioned the first humans out of clay while Oduduwa became the first divine king of the Yoruba people. Historical evidence, however, tells a different story. According to historians, the area was originally populated by the Igbo people when Oduduwa and his army invaded the city from the north, pushed the earlier inhabitants to the east, and established the first Yoruba kingdom. After the death of Oduduwa, his sons and other descendants spread out from Ife-Ife to found other Yoruba states. Eventually the Yoruba became one of Africa's largest ethnic groups. They also remain the vast majority of Ife-Ife's inhabitants. The current royal dynasty of Ile-Ife is over eight centuries old.

When I told Oby we were going to Ife, she warned me about juju. Juju was what people called the African traditional spirituality, or at least the part of it used for evil. It was difficult not to be spiritual there, drawn into the mysticism and faith of the people. They believed that there was a life-giving force present in all things, including humans, the air, rocks, and animals. This force was the spirit of the Almighty and could only be approached through lesser gods. The ancestors knew of this force, they communicated with it and lived in harmony with it. Africans were communicating with this God before the missionaries came to these shores.

Mr. Okon parked the car and informed us that he would be anointing it before we got closer to town. He anointed everything, pouring a bit olive oil while saying a prayer of protection over the car and passengers. The steering wheel, rearview mirror, even the tires and the engine got some anointing. He put a bit of oil on our luggage but Adey warned him not to soil the clothes.

We pulled into a sprawling tree-lined driveway that was almost a mile long. We drove past a lake dotted with ducks and ducklings and nestled among various trees. We identified mangoes, African star apples, tamarinds, and garden eggs, among others. The driveway to the mansion was lined with beautiful bougainvillea. Adey's dad, Prince Adepoju, was standing outside the house. This gesture itself was noteworthy as Nigerian "big men" wouldn't have waited outside their home for anyone but would rather have waited for visitors to be ushered into their presence. But there he was, waiting with the rest of the family for his son. I had imagined Adey's dad to be an older version of him. Perhaps a man in his sixties with a rounded belly and greying hair. I was ready for severe weight loss because of the cancer treatment but was pleasantly disappointed when the man that appeared before us was fit, handsome, and the spitting image of Adey. Sure, his face was a little more mature, but they were undeniably father and son.

I could imagine what had attracted Ms. Washington to this magnificent man. His swagger would have perfectly matched her extravagance. It was also a bit disappointing to see him alive and well and in this beautiful home. He wasn't poor, he wasn't dying today. What had stopped him from contacting Adey all these years?

Both men hugged; tears rolled down from Adey's eyes. We were ushered into an ornate golden room. Adey's father narrated his story. He was twenty-two when he was sent to the United States to study. He met Ms. Washington and the two of them fell in love quickly. Yes, the pregnancy was unplanned but they were both happy. For a couple of years after he finished with his first degree, he hung around, worked a couple of odd jobs. He took Adey to the park and enjoyed each moment knowing that the moment might not last. Happiness was short-lived because he was called back home by his father to face his responsibilities. One day the dreaded phone call came through. He had been betrothed since before he could walk. Somehow he had reasoned that all that would disappear once he came to the United States. But the chicken had come home to roost. Once his parents discovered his secret marriage and child in the US, they ordered him to either come home or be brought back to Nigeria forcefully. That was how he described the entire story of his son's existence. A life he left behind the minute he touched the shores of Nigeria again. He'd made sure to send money over the years but what is money to a little boy yearning for his father?

When Adey asked why he'd never reached out, he explained that it was to avoid complicating things.

"First I didn't know what to say or how to explain myself, then the days turned to months and years. Then it became too late. Son, he who doesn't find his way back from the forest gets lost in it. I hope to find my way back to you."

Adey said he understood. Later I came to realize he said this because he didn't want anything to spoil the moment he'd waited for all his life. Adey was keen to know if he had any siblings. He had a sister, who was married and lived with her family in Lagos, and a brother, who had died some months before. This revelation would bring us to an understanding of why we had been invited to Nigeria. If I was angry before, what I was about to hear would send my blood pressure through the roof.

Chapter 30

The Ooni of Ife was selected from a group of thirteen royal families who all had a right to the throne. When the time came for a new Ooni to be chosen, a secret ceremony was performed and the Ooni was selected from the representatives of the thirteen families. Adey's last name was Adepoju, meaning "the crown brings abundance." His family was one of the thirteen royal families. Prince Kunle Adepoju, Adey's father's oldest son, should have been the representative but he had died unexpected. Kunle's death meant that Adey's father wouldn't have an heir, which made ascending to the throne impossible. No one knew that he had another son, Adey, in the United States. His arrival had sent shock waves throughout the land.

Adey's father told us that during a trip to the north a few years before, he had gone with an associate to a prayer house. They'd struck a deal on the exportation of dairy products and the man required an extra level of spiritual consensus to be sure he wouldn't be swindled. This was a normal occurrence in the country. During the consultation, the priest informed Adey's father of an impending disaster in his life. The Ooni would vacate the throne and Adey's father would have no heir unless he corrected his wrong. He didn't think anything of it until years later when his son, Adey's half-brother, died. The death of his son was the reason he'd left Lagos. They were both on Third Mainland Bridge, with him driving behind, when Kunle's tire blew out. He lost control of the car and somersaulted into the Lagos Lagoon below. Adey's father swore he heard Kunle screaming

149

as the car vanished into the waters below. He broke down as he told us the story.

"When they found his body, his eyes had been eaten by fish."

He shook his head like he was trying to banish the image from his mind. Some months after Adey's father moved back to Ife, the Ooni died. He couldn't in good faith be in count for the throne because of his medical condition. He had to abdicate and pass the honor to his children. He realized it was time to call Adey home. This was the reason Adey had flown from America, not because there was a man who was dying or a man who wanted to reconnect with his son. We'd come here because Adey's father needed him to perform duties for a family he had never known. Adey was next in line to be Ooni and his entire life would change if he was selected by the oracle.

My heart broke for the little boy that had had his dreams crushed by this entitled man. Adey sat with a forlorn face after hearing this story.

"What if the Ooni hadn't died?"

Adey's father sat back in his chair. He looked Adey and said, "You are my son. You will always be my son."

I'm not sure what reaction I was expecting from Adey. With a strange meekness, he asked, "When is the ceremony?"

I was confused, why did he care? His dad replied, "It's in two weeks. But I have to tell you that this has become dangerous. You cannot leave the house because you are not safe here. I cannot afford to lose another son. People are just finding out that you exist and they are all trying to eliminate each other. Please stay here till it's all over."

That was a bit longer than we'd planned, but that wasn't the point. I couldn't understand what was happening to Adey. It wasn't the place or time for me to say anything. I just sat there, while he continued his conversation with his father. They talked about his life and the family.

In his own time, the selection had been one of the reasons Adey's father was called back to complete his marriage. His father-in-law had been business partners with his father. They wanted the deal sealed before the ceremony. Adey's stepmother wanted to make sure she was securely by her betrothed's side should he be chosen as Ooni. Clearly, he hadn't been selected and he never became Ooni. Rarely did it happen that a man witnessed two selections in his lifetime. The circumstances around the

Ooni's death now had been a huge source of speculation. The Ooni was leaving the palace when he saw a beautiful woman, Funmi, whose skin shone like the sun. The Ooni decided that she had to become his wife. It's possible the Ooni didn't know or maybe he just didn't care that Funmi was a mistress of Chief Alaga, one of the most powerful men in Ife. Shortly after the Ooni's marriage to Funmi, Chief Alaga, who was "happily" married with four kids, declared war on the Ooni. He did everything within his power to create unrest and make the town ungovernable. It was hard to pin it directly on him, but those who knew the workings of the underworld swore it was him. Just like the story of Samson and Delilah, it appeared the Ooni had leaked the secret of his power to Funmi and that was his undoing. She still walked free, for now. Adey's dad said the Ifa priests were consulting to reveal the truth. The eyes of the gods had been shrouded by powerful men.

Chief Alaga's victory over the Ooni gave him clout in the power circles. He deemed himself powerful enough to interfere with the selection because he wanted his own candidate installed.

The room had become too crowded for me and I stepped outside for some air. I saw Mr. Okon sitting by the car and I stepped towards him. We hadn't been there six hours and Mr. Okon already had the inside scoop. Adey's half-brother had allegedly been killed by a member of another family. This was a race that involved the elimination of the competition and survival of the fittest. I was exhausted, and I would have given anything to be transported back to Lagos.

Adey's dad made sure there was a room prepared for us at the house. I had no plans of sleeping there. Thankfully, Adey agreed that we should spend the night at a hotel and we were escorted by bodyguards and Ifa priests. I thought we were on the same page about everything, but as we talked, Adey made it clear he was considering partaking in this selection ritual. He thought it a privilege to be part of this tradition. He had to stand in the place of his deceased brother. There was no turning back now. As a child, he had hoped that his name meant he was a real king. He'd daydreamed of his dad calling him back one day to reclaim the throne. Adey could see I wasn't excited, he quickly consoled me that the odds were not in his favor. He simply would like to fulfill his father's wishes and then go back to his life in California. Adey was the most logical person I knew. Listening to him, I got his point. But I was scared for our safety. I was scared that his emotions were driving this decision. I was scared of the power his father had over him. By the time I realized what was happening, it was too late. The conversation was spiraling into an argument and I didn't hold back.

"This is Richard all over again!"

He looked at me like I had hit him with a ton of bricks. I continued, "You are bending to your father like a scared little boy!"

He spoke calmly, "How can you compare me to that monster?"

I picked up my hand luggage, ready to leave the room. He beat me to the door.

"No, I'll leave."

And with that, he was gone. I felt the ground slip from under me. What was Ile-Ife doing to us? I cried and waited but Adey never came back. As I lay in bed, I tried to push away all the horrible scenarios that were playing in my mind. I thought about calling someone, this would be a good time to talk to Caleb. The sound of his voice was tonic to my soul. Or should it Momma? Her voice of reason might be what I need tonight. Or Shade and Ebony or even Ms. Washington? Ultimately I decided on silence. Maybe what I needed was space to wrestle these demons that had gathered to torment me.

I wrestled with the fact that we were Christians venturing into tribal spiritual spaces. I wrestled with the possibility of being thrust into the horrible world of Nigerian politics. My main wrestle was with the reenactment of father-son manipulations. I immediately saw the Braithwaites. Another son marching to the destructive tune of his father. Adey did not get to walk out on me. He needed to make a decision. We could spend a few days with his father and then leave for Lagos as planned. If he insisted on partaking in the ceremony, I would leave immediately. I ate my breakfast nervously as I waited for Adey to arrive. Apparently he had slept in the next room. Adey walked in sometime before noon. His mind was pretty much made up when he walked in through the door. The ultimatum pushed it to a hundred percent. This was an important moment in our relationship, a turning point. I was naïve to think that for all those years we were apart Adey had stayed the same. Yes, at his core he was the same Adey from Sunset Street, but over time he had become this man before me, one willing to let me walk away. Or maybe this was who he had always been—after all, he'd let me go the first time. Wasn't this Richard all over again? Here was another man picking his father and family over me. It felt like my lights had been turned off. I couldn't breathe. Wave after wave of rejection washed over me. Adey was in pain too; I had promised to stand by him, I was here to experience this time in his life but I couldn't hear him. I couldn't hear him over the sound of my doubts and fears. He held my hand as I was about to walk out the door. In the calmest voice, he said, "Allie, please, don't do this. Please."

I could not hear him, neither could I look at him, but each time I shut my eyes, his face slammed through my panic.

Mr. Okon was uncharacteristically quiet throughout the trip back to Lagos and allowed me the space to weep silently. We were stuck in Ibadan Expressway traffic for five hours and by the time we got to the hotel, I felt a little sick. Mr. Okon recommended going to Oby's, but I needed to be alone. The shadows in my life were colluding with the dark places and dragging me along with them. If they didn't take me at night, I'd be ready to face the morning. I wrestled with myself all night. Demons that I thought had been conquered came rushing into the room. Had I done the right thing? The more I dug, the more I sank deeper into dark clouds. What if all he'd told me had been lies and he really had just moved on for all those years? What kind of man told the girl he loved to date other people and then put down every guy she met? By the time morning came around, I'd convinced myself I was in an emotionally abusive relationship and Adey was the enemy.

There was no turning back now. I was going to be on the next flight to the United States. I decided against calling anyone so I wouldn't have to explain. How would I tell Caleb that Adey wouldn't be in his life anymore? Ultimately I could not repeat the mistakes of my past.

The thing about a developing country is that it is developing. That means sometimes things simply do not work. I couldn't comprehend that all flights out of Nigeria had temporarily been suspended. The embassy said it would only be a couple of days but US citizens like me would have the opportunity to be evacuated should the lockdown last longer. Mr. Okon was happy that I couldn't leave but I did not find it humorous at all.

Chapter *31*

Thankfully, Oby wasn't in town, because I didn't want to speak to anybody. I was aware I was struggling and I needed to heal my own way. When it came down to it, I knew that God was directing the trajectory of my life. Someone had once told me that we are tested in order to be promoted. I felt like I'd had enough tests for heaven to be satisfied. How else should I prove loyalty? Or was it growth and maturity? I really didn't know what God wanted from me. I lay there in silence, hoping something would rise above the waves. I woke up with a renewed sense of purpose—I still wasn't ready to talk to anyone from home because they would ask for Adey and I didn't want to lie. Still, I ended up picking up Caleb's call.

He knew something was wrong the moment he heard my voice. There is a connection between mother and child that crosses international zones. Lying was pointless, so I told him the most censored, summarized version of what happened. He said, "Don't worry, Mommy, Amanda and I had a fight, but now we are closer. You and Mr. Adey will make-up soon."

I hoped it would be the same for Adey and me. I didn't want to put Caleb under the pressure of keeping this huge secret from everyone else. I talked to Momma first. She had many questions but she also encouraged me to take time for myself. She reasoned that Adey and I were becoming a couple and were bound to need to iron out a few kinks on the way. Pop asked if he needed to come get me. Shade and Ebony couldn't believe the Nigerian kingship was real. I was happy to have called them because I hadn't thought it was possible to laugh at this moment. Shade was having a hard time understanding my reaction but Ebony repeated a phrase she'd heard on *Oprah*, "If it's hysterical, it must be historical." Then she added, "Girl, get that checked out. Find yourself a gorgeous Lagos therapist."

Black people brush trauma under a rug. We somehow believe the color of our skin shields us from mental health issues. People like Mr. Okon and the manager at the hotel talked about their suffering like they were in a competition for the most damaged. The truth is hurt people see through foggy lenses.

Fola referred me to his therapist and this was unlike anything I'd experienced. Her office was on the fourth floor of a high-rise building in Victoria Island. I walked into an office with lush carpets and exquisite light fixtures; I was paying a substantial amount to this visit, so I expected the services to match or exceed the décor. I felt guilty for judging her too quickly. Dr. Folashade practiced African trauma care merged with a few of the modalities I practiced.

I was hooked the first day. The intake was brief and Dr. Folashade explained that the first session would culminate in a herb bath, where I would soak until healing happened. I was ready for the experience so I nodded. She then asked permission to hold my hands and made eye contact. We sat in slience for several minutes and I felt pulled into a sort of hynoptic encounter. Something cracked open and I was transported to Little Africa. I saw a little girl clothed in fear. I could see her beautiful, brightly colored lace dress but she cowered in fear. She looked happy on the outside but I saw her. I reached out to turn the little girl around so I could hug her. I wanted to give her hope and tell her all would be well. As she turned, I was stunned to see that it was me as a child. But how is that possible? I was cocooned in the love of Tolah and James Smith. This couldn't be me. Then I understood and began to wail for that child.

One of the staff immediately led me to a dimly lit gigantic bathroom and shut the door behind me. I remove my clothes and immersed myself in the bath. Lamentation dirges filled the room. As I soaked in the herb bath, I was transported back to the little girl and I saw the child Allie for the first time. It was fear that had made me curl into Momma and Pop's love so ferociously. Fear of the gangs on our streets. Fear I could be shot each time I stepped outside the house. Fear of the violence that was all around us. Someone died almost every day in Little Africa and it made me cling to the ones around me ferociously. It's why I clung to Adey and why I was still clinging. Fear is what led me to Richard. I understood myself intimately. It felt as if my soul was undergoing a cataclysmic shift. Everything was falling into place. I reached out and gave Little Allie the tightest hug. I muttered, "Nothing to fear, young one. Welcome home!" At that moment, I felt it rising like dough and it pulsated in my entire fabric. Laughter! I saw little Allie laughing and I joined in and our laughter floated into the rooms and circled like balloons at a birthday party.

I had stayed exactly sixty-three minutes in the Mourning Room, as it was called, but it felt I had been there for a year. What happened? This was stuff that I hadn't learned in my clinical PhD program. Just one session, with minimum conversation, and I had healed my wounded child. As I exited the room, I saw three smiling women sitting on a bench with big grins on their face. Immediately they looked at me, and I realized that the lamentation dirge had flowed out of them. They had gone to hell with me and journeyed back to life. I was not alone. I beamed and went to give individual hugs but they all got up and pulled me into a warm embrace.

There was no rush. No sense of timing. Dr. Folashade explained that each soul got what they needed. She also explained that she hadn't hypnotized me but had mirrored the me I was afraid to see.

"You did all the work, Allie. You can book another appointment if you feel the need, but I think you are free to live now."

She was correct! I had learned so much about myself. Adey had done me a great favor by not keeping in touch. I'd been leaning on him like a tendril incapable of standing on my own. So much of my identity had been wrapped around Adey that when we were apart, I unraveled. That was a lot of pressure on any one person. It was unfair to both of us. I changed my return ticket and stayed in Lagos. I couldn't wait to share my experience with Adey and for the first time, I truly hoped he was enjoying himself. I prayed for Adey.

I made an appointment to have my hair braided at the Lagoon Hair Shop. While Ngozi and a couple other girls were braiding, the entire shop was in silence as the voice of Hauwa pierced the silence. Hauwa was about twenty-six years old with an obvious black eye and a crying baby tied to her back. Hauwa had grown up in a village in northern Nigeria.

At eighteen years old, her single status was a problem and embarrassment for her family. Hauwa, however, had dreams of furthering her education. She came home from the farm one day to visitors in the house. She was informed that these were her husband's people and Allah had decided to be merciful to her. Her betrothed was a young man named Danku, a young okada driver in Lagos. She wasn't given an alternative and the wedding took place the next day. She was married to Danku in absentia. For three years after the wedding she lived with Danku's family. She performed all the duties of a wife in the family while waiting for her husband to visit. Finally, he showed up and the disaster started. Danku was a rugged man with red eyes who popped pain pills that made him erratic. By the time they were to leave for Lagos, she had severe bruises in her vagina and anus from repeated rapes.

When the couple arrived in Lagos, the situation got worse. The couple lived in a tiny wooden room, built on an abandoned plot of swampy land on the Lekki axis of Lagos. The drugs and raping didn't stop and she became pregnant. Her first child died of malaria. The poor child was no match for the swamp mosquitoes. She got pregnant two more times but they ended in miscarriage. She finally gave birth to her son, Ali. Now she struggled with the issue of low breast milk supply. She'd started the baby on a diet of pap, a cereal made from corn and garri, dry cassava flakes.

According to her, Danku had come home the night before with sunken eyes and a blue tongue. He was injured and told her he had lost his bike and needed money to replace it. A man had offered him N50,000 for their child and he was going to sell Ali. Her life since she'd gotten married to Danku had been a blur of beatings, starvation, and rape until Ali. She did petty trading but he spent all her profit. Hauwa had fled her house with Ali and stopped by the hair shop to say goodbye to her friend. I felt she was telling my story and I wanted to help. We went shopping for the baby. Mr. Okon was amazed that I got them a room at the George. In his words, "When person time come e go be like say na juju."

Hauwa cried and thanked me nonstop, but I was far from finished. With Fola's help, the baby buyer was arrested. I also booked Hauwa sessions with Dr. Folashade. With Fola's help, we arranged to meet with her husband, Danku, who arrived at the meeting with trepidation, not knowing quite what to expect. He listened. He pondered. You could see shame overcoming him and, in the face of his soberness, he realized the weight of the machinations, to sell his child for the price of a rented bike that could be repossessed at any time. I gave him my offer—if he was willing to commit to a treatment program, we would provide him a new bike and two others that he could rent to others. Danku was overwhelmed. He wept like a baby and knelt before his wife. Danku checked himself into the treatment center in Ikeja and stayed there for three months.

Hauwa registered for the Lagos State agriculture scheme. We paid for some an acreage in Abeokuta for Hauwa and a few other women to farm and linked them with business mentors. Years later, Hauwa and Danku were thriving. Danku became an entrepreneur with multiple projects. T o g e t h e r they headed our foundation in western Nigeria. They were proud parents of three children. Beauty from ashes. Oasis in the desert. Sunshine after the rain. Hope finds a way to stretch after a lull, shake itself up, and slowly rise into the dawn of a new day.

Perhaps I'd gone through my marriage with Richard to be able to better understand battered women. I informed my partners in Los Angeles that we would be expanding our operations to Nigeria. How could I feign ignorance after all I had seen and heard in this land?

I missed Adey and returned his calls after a few days. It was a fresh breeze to my soul. Adey and I spoke at length about everthing under the sun. Adey told me about his great-grandmother, who had been a popular Ifa priestess. She was so powerful that obas consulted her from all over the Yoruba kingdom. We talked about Ms. Washington's decision to publish a new book about her death scare and life change. With a boyish excitement, Adey told me about all the relatives he'd met and a cousin that looked so much like him everyone said they were twins. A part of me was sad he was getting on fine without me, but I was happy he was reconnecting with his roots and healing. Before he hung up, he said Ms. Washington had told him not to return to the United States without me. I laughed and said, "Goodnight."

It was Fola who called me in the early hours of the morning to tell me it was finally okay to travel, but I knew I wasn't leaving this continent without Adey. I spent the day with Oby, who was finally back from South Africa. I was certain Oby had visited every country in the world at least twice.

Chapter 32

I held my breath as Mr. Okon weaved through Lagos traffic, honking and hurling insults at whoever got in our way. I reminded him that we were better off arriving in Ife late than dead. Adey, whose stay had been prolonged due to the infighing of the families, was planning to head to Lagos in the afternoon. I was laced in hope, not fear. Adey needed to honor his father and family legacy. I'd be damned if I would be the one that took that chance from him.

I walked in as he was having breakfast. To say he was stunned to see me would be an understatement. He lifted me off the floor and was close to tears.

"What are you doing here? I was just about to leave."

I looked into his eyes and said, "I returned to you."

He kissed me right there, in front of his dad and staff. Mr. Okon was beaming; later that evening I heard him tell his wife he loved her on the phone. Adey's father was elated and made sure that I knew it. I was treated to a specially prepared traditional meal, after which he invited me to a walk around the property.

"My daughter, I don't know what happened between you and my son but remember that the quarrel of lovers is the renewal of love. When one is in love, a cliff becomes a meadow. You have retuned to my prince on the wings of love. May it sustain you."

He thanked me for allowing him to have time with his son. He spoke about his life, his regrets, and how proud he was of Adey, his prince.

He beamed proudly and told me that his son was blessed to have me in his life and that we could both count on his support in the future. Once we entered the Adepojus' mansion, Adey and the entire family were summoned to the living room. We were both asked to kneel in the center of the family. They enfolded us in prayers and powerful declarations as each elder took turns to lay hands and uttered blessings over us. Finally, Adey's dad asked us to rise and face him.

"My son has come home. I give you the rest of my life. The strength of the crocodile is in the water, may you flourish in the right environment. May the ancestors speak on your behalf. No matter how long the night, the dawn will break in your favor. May the sun not smite you. Flow like water and return to your tribe in peace."

Tears streamed down both father and son's faces. Then Adey's father turned to me and said, "Our wife!"

I showed my surprise. He placed Adey's hands in mine and gave us his blessings.

He wasn't finished because he proceeded to announce Adey as his heir apparent.

Adey decided to drive me around Ile-Ife that evening, to the chagrin of all as his life was still in danger, so we were given escorts. The silence wrapped around us for over an hour. How does one describe an awakening? How does a butterfly describe metamorphosis? All it can do is spread its wings and fly.

We took a quick trip to the Erin-Ijesha Waterfalls, located a few kilometers from Ife.

The name Erin-Ijesha can be loosely translated as "the elephant of Ijesha." At the top of the hill is the source of the water and the ancient village of Abake. There was ample parking at the base and we began a winding hike into the hills of the whispering waterfalls. Our guide shared that stories of the origins of the waterfalls were as colorful as the place itself. Some believed that the falls had been discovered by the daughter of Oduduwa, ancestral progenitor of Yorubaland. Another tale said it had been discovered during a hunting trip. They'd named the falls after a god Olumirin. I preferred the tale of the discovery by Oduduwa's daughter because it marked the presence of womanhood in this scared place. Adey and I were in awe of this place.

The waterfall itself was seven levels tall, a magnificent beauty nestled on the hillside. Adey and I challenged ourselves to make the climb, but by the fourth tier, I was exhausted. With Adey's encouragement, I made it to the top. We paused under one of the iroko trees.

Adey held my hands and said, "Forgive me, Allie Pooh!"

"No, forgive me," I responded.

He held a hand to my lips and said, "Please." Then he continued, "You are my shade and light. The light that keeps me going. I fell in love with you the moment my eyes opened to girls. It's always been you. No other compares. I wouldn't trade this moment for the world. Thank you for skating across the world with me. If I ever fall behind, Allie, please wait for me. I will catch up. My love."

"Oh, Adey, I love you. I'm sorry."

We locked in an endless embrace. It wasn't a wedding proposal but I knew this moment was locked in my cells. The lamp of love burned brighter. I held him tighter, and he pulled me closer. No more words. Just our heartbeats in tandem. I can't describe how we got home, even Mr. Okon was quiet. We were in bed together and kissed gently. I wanted him, but Adey pulled back.

"Allie, let's wait till our wedding night. I want this to be special."

I knew exactly what he meant. We'd been renewed under that iroko tree. I no longer needed reassurance that I was loved. I was enough. I could wait. I was healed. I started to laugh, and Adey joined in.

Ife was in chaos when we returned. Another one of the top contenders from a member of the thirteen families had turned up dead. He'd died in his sleep. It was unclear if they were organic supporters or a mob paid by the family, but thugs were causing mayhem in the town.

If Adey was selected as Ooni, he would be unable to turn down the crown. He would need to undergo ancient rituals that were said to transform from a man to a god, the Ooni of Ife. There were stories about the power of the Ooni, how they couldn't be photographed without their consent. It was also said that all the Ooni had to do was think about sleeping with a woman and she willingly submitted herself to him.

It was a nerve-wracking day and finally the oracle chose another family. A sigh of relief from Adey reflected my sentiments.

The next day we were on our way to Lagos. His dad thanked him profusely before we left. He even offered to send money to his mother. I guess he really had no idea how well-off Ms. Washington was. Adey said he'd carefully avoided any talk of his mother.

Concerning Adey's father's health, there wasn't much we could do; he was bent on using traditional medicine. He had a man who mixed healing herbs for him. They could be on to something.

Adey and I went property shopping. The naira was dropping in value and buying was an opportunity we couldn't resist. Adey's father had connected us with a real estate agent, a fashionable woman, Lola, who had graduated from an Ivy League school and landed a job with a top firm in Dubai. Now she was back home, serving as the head of regional operations. Our budget meant we got taken care of by the boss.

We played around with the idea of buying land and buildings; it was common for Nigerians to buy or inherit land and build. In the east, the villages were packed with sprawling mansions built by native billionaires.

Adey promised to visit his father once a year, but still it would be impossible to supervise a building project. Mr. Okon offered to help but Fola warned that the money involved will be a temptation for him. Fola had no interest in construction, so we decided to purchase a building. We visited beautiful houses in Banana Island and Old Ikoyi. Lola advised us to visit a strip mall in Lekki, after which we were handed the ownership papers. We stood in shock for a moment before it dawned on us. Adey called his dad, "Dad!"

"Son, consider it a pre-wedding gift. It is also a property that doesn't need your daily attention. I will have my people oversee it for you if you want."

"Thank you, Dad!"

Chapter 33

Adey and I walked into the biggest surprise. Oby had organized a small send-off party. Most of the faces were familiar and it was so perfect. I was glad to be there. There I was, a descendant of slaves taken from this land together with my people. I'd come back with my story of how we'd survived. Thrived even! All of us there were the portraits of the African story. We kept hope alive.

It was a fun night. We laughed and danced to Nigerian music. My body gyrated to the Afrobeat. Oby and I were seated on one of the balconies in the house, just reminiscing about our days in school. Wine flowed easily and I told Oby about what had happened with Richard. She was mortified. She cried and hugged me but I surprised myself with how calm I was. It had become a part of my story, not the story of my life.

Oby told me about the real state of her marriage to Nnamdi. They had grown distant over the years but had managed to keep some semblance of a relationship. Whatever they had left had been completely destroyed when she found out about his family in the UK. About three years after they married, Nnamdi had had a child with a woman in the UK. He'd kept this a secret for years. She couldn't leave him because his money supported her. Her business was still growing and the inflow of cash from Nnamdi went a long way. I knew it was a front; I could tell she loved Nnamdi, she always had.

He did everything to make her happy after she found out. He even took a month off work to spend time with her. She blamed herself for his infidelity. She had just started her company and was working overtime; Nnamdi took a business trip to London and had a one-night stand that turned into a baby. She admitted that nothing was the same between them because every time she looked at him, she imagined him with the other woman and a child to seal the deal. Because of him, she was harboring resentment towards an innocent child. How was she to forgive this? I didn't have any words of wisdom or advice, I just held her and let her cry. There was no manual for something like this, only time could heal this wound. Adey found us during the cry session. He had a confused look on his face and I shook my head, signaling him to give us time. I referred Oby to Dr. Pedro.

The next day, Adey and I woke up around midday and enjoyed a late breakfast at the pool. Fola was on his way to Venice so he popped in to say goodbye. I was going to miss him. He'd definitely made this trip impactful. Fola was instrumental in completing the healing circle. I thanked him from the depths of my soul. We promised to keep in touch.

I didn't know how to react when, later that day, Momma called to tell me Richard's lawyers had tried to get in touch with Caleb. My face grew hot with anger. The court ruling mandated he stay away from me. We had an agreement that he was to stay away from Caleb as well. It was not entirely shocking for a man like Richard, a man of notable wealth, to break an agreement. I was on the phone immediately with my lawyer, who assured us that nothing would come out of the filing.

Adey was almost angrier than I; he paced the room, cursing under his breath. I think it was the first time I'd heard Adey threaten to hit someone.

Ms. Washington was also upset. She ended her trip early to return home, and I wasn't sure what she planned to do.

Pop was the voice of reason, he reminded me to focus my anger on getting what I wanted. Sure, he was angry, but these were tactical people; it was best to beat them at their own game.

When I called Shade, Johnny said she was on bed rest. There had been a little bleeding and the doctors advised she stay off her feet. Ebony in her usual feisty way threatened fire and brimstone. She was ready to storm the prison and give Richard a piece of her mind. That night when I got out of the shower, Adey led me to the bed. He asked in the calmest voice, "Are you okay?"

I checked within me and found stillness. Serenity. Peace. I whispered, "He won't get out."

Adey nodded in agreement. "I won't let that happen."

We were in this together. We were armed with the strength of belonging and nothing could shake our resolve. I fell asleep in his embrace.

Mr. Okon showed up with his wife and daughter early that morning. It was embarrassing when they knelt in the lobby thanking us. Adey and I had given Mr. Okon a reasonable sum of money, after all the stories we had heard, it was impossible to leave him with nothing. His wife was dark-skinned, elegant, and tall. Their daughter looked exactly like Mr. Okon. The woman talked a lot. "Una do well o, my husband don change, now en dey talk I love you for phone, en no dey drink like before."

Mr. Okon blushed like a shy teenager as she spoke.

Their daughter thanked us. Because of us, she would be attending the boarding school of her dreams. We then offered to pay her tuition till she graduated university. Mr. Okon's wife screamed as she rolled on the floor, her long arms thrashing everywhere like someone having a seizure.

"Abasi! You say!"

Mr. Okon got her off the floor. She knelt with her palms together. Tears streamed down her cheeks.

"God go bless una, you go make plenty money, you go born plenty fine children." We thanked her for thanking us.

On the plane, there was a pregnant woman in the seat adjacent to mine who was sweating profusely and adjusting herself nervously. At some point, I got so concerned that I called the flight attendant to get her some water. Suddenly she fell, foaming at the mouth, her eyes rolling back in her head. Adey swung into action, doing his best to stabilize her. When we landed, she was rushed to a hospital. Apparently she was a mule and had swallowed balls of cocaine.

It felt good to be home. The entire village was there, Momma, Pop, Caleb, Ms. Washington, and Ebony.

Chapter 34

Shade lost the babies. They had induced labor and she'd had to push out her lifeless twins. I was broken for her, we cried on the phone together. She wanted to be alone for a couple of days, she had put so much into this and she was having a hard time. Johnny booked her a hotel. He would take care of their daughter, Zola, to give Shade time to mourn. Eb and I got the hotel name from Johnny and booked the biggest suite. We took Zola with us and loved on her while her mom and dad grieved. Shade knew we were in the same hotel and later told us it gave her comfort that we were so close. Each day we had her favorite foods sent to her room. We took Zola on a tour of Los Angeles, from Disneyland to Knott's Berry Farm to botanical gardens. We had something planned for each day and usually returned to the hotel exhausted. Zola was a joy to have and she wore us out! One night, almost a week later, we heard a knock on the door and it was Shade and Johnny. Zola screeched, "Mommy! Daddy!" Johnny picked and swirled her and handed her to Shade, who hugged her tight. Then she walked towards Eb and I as we rushed towards her. Sister love is such good medicine. She whispered, "Thank you!"

She said that she had a feeling that she wasn't meant to carry another child. Maybe this was God's way of telling her to adopt. I agreed. I reassured her that adoption was an eternal gift and didn't preclude her having her own. "Time is a gift. Let's see what it brings."

I spent a lot of time with Caleb. He was happy and his life was filled with his favorite things. I attended chess games and spelling bee finals.

Adey and I went on dates at least twice a week. He had to go out of town a few times for work but he always made sure to visit first thing once he returned.

Life went back to normal. One night I was in my parents' kitchen, loading up my plate with biscuits, when Momma walked in. She wanted to know what the plan was with Adey.

At work, Beatrice had started calling me iyawo, a Yoruba term meaning "our wife."

Maybe Beatrice was right, Nigeria had gotten under my skin. Adey and I visited Nigerian restaurants in the area, keeping up with Fola's restaurant-hopping tradition. We took Caleb with us and he found egusi soup to be his favorite. I also took notice of Caleb's culinary skills and did my best to encourage them.

For weeks, Adey had been preparing for a big surgery. A popular NGO had booked him to perform a groundbreaking surgery, a separation of conjoined twins. Adey was a nervous mess. The team spent hours at the hospital preparing and the whole world was watching. The twins had featured on a popular TV program that showcased unique disabilities. Adey became a celebrity overnight, he was like a boxer preparing for a game. Marshawn helped coach him on answering questions. Finally, they had something to bond over.

I sat in the hospital lobby for the entire thirty-seven hours of the surgery. I knew if the tables had been turned, he would have done the same for me. Every time an update came through, my heart would skip a beat. I could only imagine how the parents felt. Somewhere around the thirty-second hour, they were losing one of the babies, but in the end they both pulled through. It was a media circus. A young Black doctor was being celebrated all over the country. Adey's face was plastered on every news report. During the news update, he gave all the credit to the team and then looked into the camera and said, "I'm coming home, Allie!"

Ms. Washington was the proudest parent alive. She told every single audience about Adey's achievements. She was also home more. Adey told me that they'd finally talked about his dad and she'd admitted how in love she'd been, how his leaving had broken her and she was never able to find love that way again.

Chapter *35*

I t was Sunday afternoon and as usual, Caleb and I were at my parents' house. We usually returned there after church and spent the rest of the day. Ms. Washington had arrived from the United Kingdom. As was her habit, she had dropped by their home to share stories. We were on the patio listening to Ms. Washington talk about a scandalous potential royal divorce.

"So much sorrow and disruption if they divorce," she lamented.

"Like Mommy and Dad?" Caleb asked.

"Do you feel sorrow and disruption?" Ms. Washington queried.

"It's okay, I've had this talk with Mommy and the therapist too. I like being with all of you. I don't miss my dad as I should because he was hardly around anyway. He was mean to Mommy and I don't like that. Mommy says that I have to forgive him."

"Yes, you do in your own time," Ms. Washington continued.

"I like that! I'm waiting for my own time to forgive him."

"Take all the time you need. Meanwhile keep loving and growing so I can take you to see the queen of England."

"I would like to see the royal family!" Caleb said.

"It's time you came with me to see the queen." Ms. Washington responded as if she had an open invitation to the court, but we'd all learned never to underestimate her. She had met presidents and luminaries one only watched on television.

Hopefully, we'd created an environment for Caleb to thrive. His father would spend the rest of his life in prison for killing his parents. Caleb's trust was worth over $100 million and he owned all the Braithwaites' properties. Caleb was studious and wanted to be a neurosurgeon like Adey. They played basketball together, a sport the Braithwaites had prevented him from participating in because it was too Black. I didn't realize that I was smiling until Caleb said, "Mommy, you are happy. I love it when you smile."

He ran over to me and gave me the tightest hug.

"I love you too, baby. You make me smile always!"

Just then Adey's car pulled up into the driveway and Caleb ran to hug him as he stepped out of the car. These two adored each other and it made my heart glad each time I witnessed the spontaneous love Caleb had for Adey.

"Hello, little man!"

"Hello, Doc!"

Adey picked him up and threw him to the ground as they pretend to wrestle. Caleb always won these battles and he loved stepping on Adey, while he laid on the ground, to declare victory.

The two grandmas were talking about European attractions. Caleb had started calling Ms. Washington Grandma, which she absolutely loved.

"Grandma! Doc is here! Grandpa! Doc is here!"

"Hello, Doc," Pop teased.

"Hello, Mr. and Mrs. Smith! Mom!"

We hugged and welcomed Adey like we hadn't just seen him yesterday. It was amazing how many hugs were doled out in this family. The house was bustling like it was Thanksgiving. The guys played basketball in the backyard. I sat with Momma and Ms. Washington.

I noticed that Cecilia was helping in the kitchen, which was not unusual for Sunday afternoons. She did that when we had a big gathering, like today, even at my parents' house. Cecilia made some jollof rice and fried plantain for Adey, who had acquired a taste for Nigerian food at Harvard. The table was spread with barbecued ribs, grilled salmon, lobster, smoked salmon, and prawns. A lot of different salads. There was roast beef and chicken with all the trimmings. A good selection of deserts was set on a separate table and I warned Caleb not to venture there until after his meal.

"Everything looks delicious! Let's eat," Momma announced.

"I hope Shade, Johnny, Marshawn, and Ebony make it on time," I mused.

"I'm sure they will be here," Adey said.

As if on cue, the doorbell rang. Adey opened the door and Ebony, Marshawn, and their son, Marshawn Junior, were there, along with Shade and Johnny and their daughter, Zola. The next generation—Junior, Zola, and Caleb—were about the same age and they got along quite well. Ebony's mom and stepdad showed up together. They had remained friends and Ebony said they were better not married. Shade's mom and her new boyfriend also came later.

The girls and I got in our circle while the others hugged and laughed and hugged some more and laughed some more.

"Pull up a chair, girls!" invited Ebony's mother.

"Well, Mom, we are not girls anymore. We are women now," Ebony said in jest.

Laughter erupted again.

I loved everything about this moment and was grateful to be a part of this family gathering. I only hoped we would continue it for all our sakes.

After dinner, we took our dessert, which consisted of peach cobbler, apple pies, and ice cream, to the living room.

"Do you remember that time when we drove cross-country?" Ebony said.

"It wasn't cross-country, missy. It was to San Francisco," Shade corrected.

"It felt like cross-country."

"And Adey held Allie's hands in between the seats like we didn't see them."

"Y'all held hands?" Ms. Washington yelled.

"Right under our noses," Momma interjected.

Adey had been quiet throughout all the banter but then he suddenly got up and said, "May I have all your attention please?"

"Why are you so serious?" Ebony teased.

"Shissh, Ebony, Adey looks tense!" Shade smacked her jokingly.

I wondered why Adey was so tense.

"Oh, I see that's how we roll today," Eb responded.

Adey continued, "I have something to say. According to Chinua Achebe, 'a man who calls his kinsmen to a feast does not do so to save them from starving. They all have food in their own homes. When we gather together in the moonlit village ground it is not because of the moon. Every man can see it in his own compound. We come together because it is good for kinsmen to do so.' I am glad that we are all kinsmen and that you are here today."

I have a story to tell and it started when I was six years old in a beautiful house on Sunset Street."

I realized what was about to happen.

He continued. "When I was ten years old, Mr. Smith asked me to take care of his daughter, Alero, Allie Pooh to me. I endeavored to do that until I left for Harvard and again since we've reconnected. Allie Pooh is my life and I can no longer live without her. I don't want to be without her again. You all know all she went through yet she stands here among us today, healing, thriving, and making miracles. Last week, I asked Pop's permission to propose to his daughter and he said yes. I also asked Caleb and he said yes!"

The whole place erupted with cheers and jubilation.

"Caleb, you knew about this?" I was genuinely surprised.

"Yes, Mommy," he said, just like a grownup!

Momma looked at Pop and smiled. Ms. Washington was also in on the surprise. Everyone was excited and waiting to celebrate but Adey was taking his moment.

Adey walked up to where I was sandwiched between Ebony and Shade, got on both knees, took out a box, and opened it. I saw the most beautiful ring in its simplicity.

"Allie Pooh, we've clocked many hours since Sunset Street. You've become my time gauge—my North Star. I want to nest with you, Caleb, and the future members of our tribe. Will you share life with me as my perfectly fitted soul?"

"Awwwwwh!" everyone screeched. The ladies were all tearing up.

"Answer him . . ."

"If y'all keep quiet," I teased.

"Adey Adepoju! What an enduring love! Our elders say that love is never lost but kept. I don't remember a moment I didn't love you. I am honored to walk this life with you. The answer is yes!"

Then he started screaming, "She said yes!" Adey picked me up and held me for what seemed like eternity. Tears streamed down both our faces.

Ms. Washington pulled me into her warm embrace, with tears rolling down her face, too. Then she began to sing "Amazing Grace" as my parents hugged Adey and then me and both of us and Caleb together. Everyone folded in this circle of home and joined the song, "I was once lost but now I'm found."